献给河北大学历史学院
专业英语课程的学生们

A Dedication to
My Students Majoring in History

河北大学中国史“双一流”学科建设经费资助

Selected Poems of Tang Dynasty 唐诗英译

Translated by Liu Yan 刘研 译

河北大学出版社
·保定·

出 版 人：朱文富
责任编辑：王红梅
装帧设计：赵　谦
责任校对：李　易
责任印制：常　凯

图书在版编目（CIP）数据

唐诗英译 ：汉英对照 / 刘研译 . -- 保定 ：河北大学出版社，2023.11
ISBN 978-7-5666-2160-3

Ⅰ . ①唐… Ⅱ . ①刘… Ⅲ . ①唐诗－诗集－汉、英 Ⅳ . ① I222.742

中国国家版本馆 CIP 数据核字 (2023) 第 231448 号

唐诗英译
TANGSHI YINGYI

出版发行：河北大学出版社
地址：河北省保定市七一东路2666号　邮编：071000
电话：0312-5073003　0312-5073029
网址：www.hbdxcbs.com
邮箱：hbdxcbs818@163.com
印　　刷：保定市北方胶印有限公司
幅面尺寸：170 mm × 230 mm
字　　数：150千字
印　　张：12.5
版　　次：2023年11月第1版
印　　次：2023年11月第1次印刷
书　　号：ISBN 978-7-5666-2160-3
定　　价：68.00 元

自 序

我曾为历史专业本科学生讲授专业英语课程。我认为学生的英语写作练习至关重要，然而，当学生数量众多且他们的写作篇幅较长时，教师很难进行充分而细致的批改。为了解决这个问题，我采用了一种办法：让学生翻译一首古诗，并为他们的作品进行批改和评分。如果学生对分数不满意，他们可以继续翻译另一首诗，直到达到他们自己满意的分数为止。这样反复进行，教师的工作量是弹性的，而学生的进步将得到有效见证。为了批改作业，我翻译了一些唐诗作为参考答案。在结束这门课程后，我继续进行翻译工作，并从所有的译文中挑选出了54位诗人的150首诗，将它们组合成了这本书。

翻译所需的字斟句酌加深了我对唐诗的理解，使我的许多解读与前人不同。上海辞书出版社1983年首次出版的《唐诗鉴赏辞典》（以下简称《鉴赏》）具有相当的影响力，不断重印和再版，互联网上也往往采用该辞书的解释，我也从中受益良多。但在字词的释义、句子的结构、意象的使用，乃至全诗的理解这几个方面，我都与《鉴赏》有一些分歧。下面我举几个例子：

1. 对于王勃《滕王阁诗》里的“佩玉鸣鸾罢歌舞”，《鉴赏》说：“想当年，建阁的滕王驾着鸾铃马车，挂着琳琅玉佩，来到阁上，举行宴会；如今，他已死去，那种豪华的场面，已经一去不复返了。”这个解释错在把“罢”理解成了“结束”。实际上，“罢”通“疲”，“罢歌舞”是指疲于歌舞。后面“画栋”和“珠帘”两句里，云飞过画栋，雨卷动珠帘，都是阁内视角，说明阁还不是空阁，从早到晚都有人，盛况仍在。

2. 对于张九龄《望月怀远》里的“灭烛怜光满，披衣觉露滋”，《鉴赏》说：“竟夕相思不能入睡，怪谁呢？是屋里烛光太耀眼吗？于是灭烛，披衣步出门庭，光线还是那么明亮。……夜已深了，气候更凉一些了，露水也沾湿了身上的衣裳。”《鉴赏》未能识别出这两句都是颠倒了语序，把原因后置。“怜（月）光满”所以“灭烛”，这里的“光满”是月光满，而非“烛光太耀眼”。“觉露滋”所以“披衣”，这也是生活常识。另外，披衣“步出门庭”在诗中没有根据。

3. 对于王昌龄《从军行》，《鉴赏》说：“读唐代边塞诗，往往因为诗中所涉及的地名古今杂举、空间悬隔而感到困惑。”我觉得，古人写诗，好像今人拍电影，为了效果，到处取景，集中呈现。不把地名当作实指，就能消除许多困惑。

4. 对于张继《枫桥夜泊》里的“江枫渔火对愁眠”，《鉴赏》说：“‘江枫’与‘渔火’，一静一动。”我觉得“枫”字的关键是“风”。《说文解字》说：“枫，枫木也。厚叶弱枝，善摇。”“枫”可以泛指风中摇动的植物。因为有风，才选择桥下避风“夜泊”。因为风的扰动，才有“乌啼”。因风而冷，才有“霜满天”。风让植物摇动，让渔火飘忽，让人失眠。可以说，“风”是理解全诗的关键。“江枫”和“渔火”并非“一静一动”，而是都在风中不安地动。

我的这些理解，都融入了英译之中，这使英译作为唐诗释义的一部分有了独到价值。此外，我的英译力求在充分理解唐诗的基础上，摆脱唐诗的汉语形态带给英译的束缚，使唐诗重生出诗意的英语形态。下面我就摆脱汉语束缚，举一些诗词英译方面的例子：

1. 省略。汉语里的许多虚指，不必落实，而可以省略。例如李白《行路难》里的“金樽清酒斗十千，玉盘珍羞直万钱”，“十千”和“万钱”都是夸张的虚指，不必译为 ten thousand coins，而可以根据需要，译成“许多钱”（a lot of money）或者“非常贵”（very costly）。又如宋代李清照《声声慢·寻寻觅觅》里的“三杯两盏淡酒”，“三杯两盏”是虚指，意思是喝了一点酒。译文不必落实为 three or two cups of light wine 或 three cups of thin wine，译为 a little thin wine 就足够了。

2. 补充。为了方便在英语世界传播，英译本身应该力求一目了然。因此，英译时可以对唐诗原文做些补充。例如“函谷”可以补充 pass，译为 Hangu Pass，以表明是个关口。“天台”可以补充 mount，译为 Mount Tiantai，以表明是座山。又如“庄生”可以补充 the thinker，译为 the thinker Zhuang，以表明身份。

3. 取舍。有些汉语元素是无法完全转译的，例如双关语。“梧桐”在汉语诗词中经常出现，因为“梧桐”谐音“无同”，表示孤独。对于“梧桐”，tung，plane，the wutong trees，the kola nut，或者 phoenix tree，所有这些译法，都会把读者的关注引向树种，而遗漏了孤独。我认为“孤独”更加重要，所以选择译为 lonely tree。而如宋代叶绍翁《夜书所见》里的“夜深篱落一灯明”，虽然“篱落”谐音“离落”，但似乎翻译时只能保住作为物质实体的“篱落”，而需牺牲作为情感体验的“离落”。

4. 重组。在把握原诗宗旨的基础上，可以尝试将原诗拆散，将意象重新组合。例如柳宗元《江雪》里的“孤舟蓑笠翁，独钓寒江雪”，我译为 On a boat, in a cape, under a hat, / Angling among snowflakes, a man old。这个译法使“孤舟蓑笠”部分变得整齐，而以“翁”结尾也别致。

以上所谈“省略”“补充”“取舍”“重组”，都是为摆脱汉语束缚而做的努力。它们往往是被“押韵”和“控制句子长度”逼迫出来的。可以说，英译过程中最费心血、最花时间的，就是“押韵”和“控制句子长度”。我顽强地追求这两个方面，即使面对许多长诗，我也争取句子的押韵和匀称。所有这些心血和时间，都是为了捕捉唐诗获得诗意的英语形态的那一刻，那蝉蜕羽化的一刻。然而“诗意”无法举例说明，只能交给大家去品味。

最后还要补充一点：即使不押韵，也能够获得音乐和形式的美。例如《杳杳寒山道》（*A Path Through the Cold Mountains is Far and Far*）：

A path through the cold mountains is far and far.
The shores of a chilly stream are dull and dull.
Birds'twitters come out here or there.
Environment it is quite a quiet.
Winds blow my face from time to time.
Snowflakes fall on me one by one.
The sun cannot be seen day after day.
The spring cannot be felt year after year.

目 录

李世民
Li Shimin

冬狩

烈烈寒风起，惨惨飞云浮。
霜浓凝广隰，冰厚结清流。

A Hunt in Winter

Cold winds cry,
And torn clouds fly.
Dense frosts harden marshes,
And thick ices locked rivers.

金鞍移上苑，玉勒骋平畴。
旌旗四望合，罝罗一面求。
楚踣争兕殪，秦亡角鹿愁。
兽忙投密树，鸿惊起砾洲。
骑敛原尘静，戈回岭日收。

Through the woods move golden saddles,
And on the plain run jade bridles.
Flags from all sides close in,
While a trap on one side is ready.
Like Chu a fighting bull dies,
And like Qin a stabbing deer cries.[1]
Hurried animals rush into the dark forest,
And feared geese fly off the stony bank.
The dust settles when we retreat steeds,
And the sun sets when we return spears.

1. Chu（楚）and Qin（秦）were two powers in Chinese history.

心非洛汭逸，意在渭滨游。
禽荒非所乐，抚辔更招忧。

Resting by the Luo River is not my hope,
While touring along the Wei River is what I want.[2]
The decrease of quarries makes me unhappy,
And the idleness of steeds is my worry.

2. Both the Luo River（洛河）and the Wei River（渭河）are tributaries of the Yellow River（黄河）.

送杜少府之任蜀川

王勃

Wang Bo

城阙辅三秦，风烟望五津。
与君离别意，同是宦游人。
海内存知己，天涯若比邻。
无为在歧路，儿女共沾巾。

Seeing Minister Steward Du off to Take Office in Shu [1]

Watching towers guard Qin's counties.
Flowing clouds surround Shu's ferries. [2]
Here and now we have to be apart,
Since we are officials under command.
No place is remote on the earth,
If there is a friend of real worth.
Hesitation at a crossing is unnecessary,
Let alone weeping like a girl or a boy.

1. The Minister Steward, or Shaofu (少府) was an office in Han Dynasty. People in this office could often see the emperor. In Tang Dynasty, it was not a real office but a high compliment.
2. Shu was an ancient state adjoining Qin and conquered by Qin. Nowadays, Shu and Qin are used to indicate areas belong to Sichuan Province and Shaanxi Province separately.

滕王阁诗

滕王高阁临江渚，佩玉鸣鸾罢歌舞。
画栋朝飞南浦云，珠帘暮卷西山雨。
闲云潭影日悠悠，物换星移几度秋。
阁中帝子今何在？槛外长江空自流。

The Prince Teng Tower[1]

The Prince Teng had built this high tower overlooking that river. [2]
Men of wealth and honor came to enjoy singing and dancing here.
Painted beams flew with the morning clouds rising from the south shores.
Pearl curtains mingled with the dusk rain falling into the west mountains.
Day after day the leisurely clouds watched their own shadows in the water.
Year after year the mansions moved on and many things changed forever.
Nowadays we cannot meet His Highness any more.
But the long river beyond rails is flowing as before.

1. Prince Teng was Li Yuanying（李元婴）, the younger brother of Emperor Taizong of Tang. He built this tower in 653. Wang Bo attended a banquet held by the Governor of Hongzhou（洪州）in the rebuilt Prince Teng Tower. His extemporization boosted his fame and made the Prince Teng Tower one of the Four Great Towers of China. The other three are the Yueyang Tower（岳阳楼）, the Yellow Crane Tower（黄鹤楼）and the Stork Tower（鹳雀楼）.
2. The river west to the Prince Teng Tower is nowadays named Gan River（赣江）, which flows south to north.

山中

长江悲已滞，万里念将归。
况属高风晚，山山黄叶飞。

In the Mountains

Before a long river I stop.
My hometown is still far-off.
Dead leaves of all mountains
Fly in the high winds of dusk.

杨炯

Yang Jiong

从军行

烽火照西京，心中自不平。
牙璋辞凤阙，铁骑绕龙城。
雪暗凋旗画，风多杂鼓声。
宁为百夫长，胜作一书生。

The Military

Beacon fires shone on the Western Capital.[1]
Feverish hearts couldn’t be calmed down.
An order was issued from the Court Imperial.
Iron steeds soon besieged the enemy’s town.
Chaotic winds had all drumbeats disturbed.
Tattered flags were dim in the heavy snow.
I’d rather be a leader of one hundred
Than be one reader of many a scroll.

1. The Western Capital of Tang was Chang’an（长安）, and the Eastern Capital was Luoyang（洛阳）.

于易水送人一绝

骆宾王

Luo Binwang

此地别燕丹，壮士发冲冠。
昔时人已没，今日水犹寒。

Farewell by the Yi River [1]

Here he left the Prince Dan.
His irate hair pushed his hat away.
Has gone off the past man.
But the river is still so cold today.

1. Luo Binwang is grouped with Wang Bo（王勃）, Yang Jiong（杨炯）and Lu Zhaolin（卢照邻）as the Four Literary Eminences in Early Tang（初唐四杰）. His "Farewell by the Yi River"was written about Jing Ke（荆轲）, who was a retainer of Crown Prince Dan of Yan State and renowned for his failed assassination attempt of Ying Zheng（嬴政）of Qin State, who later became Qin Shi Huang（秦始皇）, China's first emperor. Before fording the Yi River（易水）, Jing Ke sang to Prince Dan that "The wind is howling and the river is cold. The hero is leaving and will not go home!"（风萧萧兮易水寒，壮士一去兮不复还）

咏鹅

鹅鹅鹅，曲项向天歌。
白毛浮绿水，红掌拨清波。

Goose

Goose, goose and goose,
Curve your neck and sing skywards.
White feathers float on the green water.
Red webs push against the clean current.

登幽州台歌

陈子昂
Chen Zi'ang

前不见古人，
后不见来者。
念天地之悠悠，
独怆然而涕下！

Upon the Youzhou Tower [1]

I see no predecessor ahead,
And no successor behind.
Between the wide earth and high sky,
Only left is my sad cry.

1. Youzhou Tower was built by King Zhao of Yan State（燕昭王）during the Warring States Period. Gold was stored on the tower for the purpose of recruiting talents. Then the talent Yue Yi（乐毅）helped Yan State defeat Qi State.

杳杳寒山道

杳杳寒山道，落落冷涧滨。
啾啾常有鸟，寂寂更无人。
淅淅风吹面，纷纷雪积身。
朝朝不见日，岁岁不知春。

A Path Through the Cold Mountains is Far and Far

A path through the cold mountains is far and far.
The shores of a chilly stream are dull and dull.
Birds'twitters come out here or there.
Environment it is quite a quiet.
Winds blow my face from time to time.
Snowflakes fall on me one by one.
The sun cannot be seen day after day.
The spring cannot be felt year after year.

咏柳

贺知章

He Zhizhang

碧玉妆成一树高，万条垂下绿丝绦。
不知细叶谁裁出，二月春风似剪刀。

A Willow Tree

This tree looks like a huge green jade.
It droops thousands of silky ribbons.
By whom are these slim leaves made?
The early spring wind is a pair of scissors.

回乡偶书

少小离家老大回，乡音无改鬓毛衰。
儿童相见不相识，笑问客从何处来。

A Note on Homecoming

When young I left home, I'm back when old.
My accent does remain, but my hair doesn't.
Children look at me, not knowing about me.
"Where are you from", they smile and inquire.

春江花月夜

张若虚

Zhang Ruoxu

春江潮水连海平，海上明月共潮生。
滟滟随波千万里，何处春江无月明。
江流宛转绕芳甸，月照花林皆似霰。
空里流霜不觉飞，汀上白沙看不见。

The Spring River and the Moonlight Flowers

The tide of spring river extends to the sea.
Along with the sea tide a bright moon rises.
It shines on all places of the spring river.
Sparkling ripples spread thousands of miles.
The winding river goes round a fragrant land.
Flowery trees here are frozen by the moonlight.
Did the ice particles flow in the air secretly?
Truly invisible on the shore is the white sand.

江天一色无纤尘，皎皎空中孤月轮。
江畔何人初见月，江月何年初照人？
人生代代无穷已，江月年年只相似。
不知江月待何人，但见长江送流水。

The river and the sky are of one pure color.
Clean and clear the lonely moon is in the air.
Which one firstly saw the moon by the river?
When did the moon shine on someone first?
Births and deaths made an endless story of people.
Year after year the moon looks same as before.
It's unknown whom the moon is waiting for.
We can only see that the river never stands still.

白云一片去悠悠，青枫浦上不胜愁。
谁家今夜扁舟子，何处相思明月楼？
可怜楼上月徘徊，应照离人妆镜台。
玉户帘中卷不去，捣衣砧上拂还来。
此时相望不相闻，愿逐月华流照君。
鸿雁长飞光不度，鱼龙潜跃水成文。

A piece of white cloud has left for a long time.
Windy trees on the shore are full of sorrow.
Whose man still floats in a tiny boat tonight?
Who misses him on a high tower in the moonlight?
The moon above the tower moves slowly and sadly.
Perhaps it shines on a dressing mirror of a lonely lady.
It cannot be rolled up in the curtain of a jade boudoir.
Or be wiped off from the board for pounding clothes.
Now she thinks of him but has no news about him.
She wants to shine on him just like a light beam.
Unlike the moonlight, a swan has to fly for a long time.
And a fish must constantly dive into and jump out of.

昨夜闲潭梦落花，可怜春半不还家。
江水流春去欲尽，江潭落月复西斜。
斜月沉沉藏海雾，碣石潇湘无限路。
不知乘月几人归，落月摇情满江树。

In a dream of last night, a flower fells into a quiet pond.
It's so sad that after a half spring he's still not back.
The spring goes with the river and will soon reach an end.
The moon above the river and the pond also falls west.
The west moon falls deeper and hides in the sea fog.
Between Jieshi and Xiaoxiang there has many a long road. [1]
Could someone get home before the moon's set?
Thereafter, only waving trees by the riverside are left.

1. Jieshi（碣石）is a mountain confronting the sea in now Changli County（昌黎县）of northeastern Hebei Province. Xiaoxiang（潇湘）refers to "lakes and rivers" region mainly in now Hunan Province. The distance between these two places was considered very long in ancient times.

望月怀远

张九龄

Zhang Jiuling

海上生明月，天涯共此时。
情人怨遥夜，竟夕起相思。
灭烛怜光满，披衣觉露滋。
不堪盈手赠，还寝梦佳期。

Gazing on the Moon and Thinking of the Absent

A bright moon rises out of the sea.
All the world shares this moment.
Missing him throughout the night,
A faraway lover falls into her grief.
She extinguishes the candle for the moonlight is enough.
She wraps herself in a dress as the dew seeps through.
Releasing the moon's sorrowful giving,
She wants to dream of a possible meeting.

登鹳雀楼

白日依山尽，黄河入海流。
欲穷千里目，更上一层楼。

Ascending the Stork Tower [1]

The white sun lingers along the ridge.
The Yellow River flows into the sea.
In order to see the most vast scenery,
We shall first get on a higher storey.

1. Among the Four Great Towers of China, only the Stork Tower was located in the north. It was located nearby Puzhou（蒲州）ancient town, now Yongji City（永济市）of Shanxi Province.

凉州词

黄河远上白云间，一片孤城万仞山。
羌笛何须怨杨柳，春风不度玉门关。

A Song of Liangzhou [1]

The Yellow River goes far into the white clouds.
A little and lonely fort lies among thousands of peaks.
Why does a nomad's flute complains with Willow Twig? [2]
The spring wind never passes through the Jade Gate. [3]

1. The area of Liangzhou (凉州 , literally: "cold and poor place") varied in different dynasties, but its core was located in east Hexi Corridor (河西走廊) , north to the Qilian Mountains (祁连山) . Liangzhou here represents all northwest frontiers.
2. Willow Twig was an ancient tune sang for parting.
3. Jade Gate (玉门关) , or Yumen Pass, is a pass of the Great Wall and the west end of Hexi Corridor. The Yellow River is very far from Jade Gate. In this poem, the Yellow River represents all rivers, and Jade Gate represents all frontier passes.

孟浩然
Meng Haoran

望洞庭湖赠张丞相

八月湖水平，涵虚混太清。
气蒸云梦泽，波撼岳阳城。
欲济无舟楫，端居耻圣明。
坐观垂钓者，徒有羡鱼情。

A Poem on the Dongting Lake Offered up to the Prime Minister Zhang [1]

The lake is full in the middle of autumn.
It reflects the Pure and connects the Empty. [2]
Its vapor envelops the marshes of Yunmeng, [3]
And waves shake up the Yueyang City. [4]
It's a shame to idle about in a great time.
But I'm sorry for having no boat to ferry.
Watching those fishers get their income,
All I can do is wait and envy.

1. Dongting Lake is a large, shallow lake in northeastern Hunan Province. The Prime Minister Zhang was Zhang Jiuling（张九龄）.In order to be recommended by him, Meng Haoran（孟浩然）wrote this poem.
2. Both the Pure and the Empty mean the sky.
3. The marshes of Yunmeng（云梦泽）,or the marshes of Cloud Dream, lying to the north of the Dongting Lake, have faded away.
4. Yueyang（岳阳）is a city on the shore of Dongting Lake.

春晓

春眠不觉晓，处处闻啼鸟。
夜来风雨声，花落知多少。

A Spring Morning

Sleep deep in spring.
Birds tell the morning.
In the storm of last night,
How many flowers did alight?

宿建德江

移舟泊烟渚，日暮客愁新。
野旷天低树，江清月近人。

Mooring on the Jiande River [1]

I moor my boat to a misty islet.
My sorrow arises anew at sunset.
The sky over the wilds is lower than a tree.
A moon in the clean river is so close to me.

1. The Jiande River is a river near to Jiande in now Zhejiang Province.

出塞

秦时明月汉时关，万里长征人未还。
但使龙城飞将在，不教胡马度阴山。

Marching Out

The moon of Qin and the fort of Han were left,
People in the long long march have not returned.
If the Flying General of Dragon Town were here, [1]
The barbarians outside Yin Mountains would not come over. [2]

1. Dragon Town, or Lulong（卢龙）, is in now northeastern Hebei Province. General Li Guang（李广）of Han Dynasty had guarded here and was called Flying General by his enemy.
2. The Yin Mountains, or Yin Shan（阴山）, is in the Inner Mongolia Autonomous Region, northern China. The Yin Mountains are a mountain range stretching across about 1000 kilometers of northern China. They form the southeastern border of the Gobi Desert and cross the Inner Mongolia Autonomous Region and Hebei Province.

从军行

青海长云暗雪山，孤城遥望玉门关。
黄沙百战穿金甲，不破楼兰终不还。

The Military

The long clouds of Green Sea shadow the snowy mountains.
A lonely castle named Jade Gate can be seen in the distance. [1]
Countless fights in the yellow sands have metal armors torn.
The warriors will not return until the Loulan City is taken. [2]

1. Green Sea, or Qinghai Lake（青海）, located in now the Qinghai Province, is the largest lake in China. The snowy mountains lying north to the Green Sea is the Qilian Mountains（祁连山）, which is to the south of Hexi Corridor. Attacking and incorporating Tuyuhun（吐谷浑）in 7 century, Tubo（吐蕃）occupied the region of Green Sea and began to threaten Hexi Corridor.
2. Loulan（楼兰）was an ancient kingdom based around an important oasis city along the Silk Road（丝绸之路）already known in the 2nd century BC. It has declined before Tang Dynasty and ended in 630.

芙蓉楼送辛渐

寒雨连江夜入吴，平明送客楚山孤。
洛阳亲友如相问，一片冰心在玉壶。

Seeing Xin Jian off at the Hibiscus Pavilion [1]

Last night, the cold rain joined the river and flowed toward Wu. [2]
At dawn, you will leave the lonely me and the mountains of Chu.
Please tell my friends and relatives in the Eastern Capital,
That my heart is a piece of ice kept in a crystal vessel. [3]

1. Xin Jian （辛渐）was a friend of Wang. Hibiscus Pavilion（芙蓉楼）was in Longbiao（龙标）of Tang, which is now the Qiancheng Town（黔城镇）of Hunan Province.
2. Wu（吴）refers to a region whose core area is around Lake Tai（太湖）. Wang had been an official in Jiangning（江宁）of Wu, then, he was demoted to Longbiao, which was in the region of Chu.
3. The crystal vessel refers to the Chinese Hu（壶）made by white jade. A very influential official of Tang Dynasty and Wu Zetian's Zhou Dynasty, Yao Chong（姚崇）, had wrote an essay named "The Warning of Icy Hu" （《冰壶诫》）to advocate the incorrupt personality. Wang agreed with him in this poem.

王维
Wang Wei

九月九日忆山东兄弟

独在异乡为异客，每逢佳节倍思亲。
遥知兄弟登高处，遍插茱萸少一人。

On the Ninth Day of the Ninth Month I Miss My Brothers to the East of Mount Hua [1]

Staying alone as a stranger in a strange land,
I miss my family even more on each festival.
My faraway brothers must have mounted high.
They all wear cornel twigs but I'm not there.

1. Wang Wei was the eldest of five brothers. Mount Hua（华山）is the western mountain of the Five Great Mountains of China（五岳）. The hometown of Wang Wei, Puzhou（蒲州）, lies to the east of Mount Hua. The Ninth Day of the Ninth Month is Double Ninth Festival or Double Yang Festival（重阳节）. According to the *Book of Changes*（《易经》）, nine is a solar number or Yang number（阳数）. Double Ninth Festival has too much Yang and is thus a potentially dangerous date. To protect against danger, it is customary to mount on a high mountain, drink chrysanthemum liquor, and wear the branches of cornel or zhuyu（茱萸）.

使至塞上

单车欲问边，属国过居延。
征蓬出汉塞，归雁入胡天。
大漠孤烟直，长河落日圆。
萧关逢候骑，都护在燕然。

Being Accredited to the Frontier

Being accredited to the frontier,
I travel far by a single carriage.
A weed rolls out of Han's area.
A goose returns to the sky savage.
One smoke in the vast desert is straight.
The sun toward a long river is round.
At a station I meet the cavalry in wait,
The Protector is still on battleground.

陇西行

十里一走马，五里一扬鞭。
都护军书至，匈奴围酒泉。
关山正飞雪，烽火断无烟。

The West of Lǒng Mountains[1]

So fast a new horse runs,
But it still should be whipped.
A Letter of Protector arrives: [2]
Jiuquan has been besieged. [3]
Over the frontier it snows.
The beacon fires die out.

1. The Lǒng Mountains（陇山）are now the dividing line of Shaanxi Province and Gansu Province.
2. Protector（都护）was the chief of Protectorate of the Western Regions（西域都护府）, which was an imperial administration imposed by Han Dynasty on many smaller states in Western Regions.
3. Jiuquan（酒泉）, or Alcohol Spring, got its name from a legendary story of the young Han general Huo Qubing（霍去病）, who was said to have poured a vat of precious alcohol into a local creek to share its taste with his troops after a victory over the Xiongnu nomads.

终南别业

中岁颇好道，晚家南山陲。
兴来每独往，胜事空自知。
行到水穷处，坐看云起时。
偶然值林叟，谈笑无还期。

My Retreat by the South Mountains [1]

When middle-aged I attended to Tao.
By the South Mountains now I house.
In high spirits I often hike alone,
Many fine scenes are shared by none.
After reaching a brook's head.
I sit waiting for the clouds to raise.
If encountering an old woodman,
I'll chat with him and not go back.

1. The South Mountains（南山）, or the Zhongnan Mountains（终南山或中南山）, are a branch of the Qin Mountains（秦岭）located in Shaanxi Province. They are an important place for Daoist hermits. Due to the mountains'close proximity to the ancient capital of Chang'an, officials who incurred the imperial court's wrath often fled to these mountains to escape punishment.

送元二使安西

渭城朝雨浥轻尘，客舍青青柳色新。
劝君更尽一杯酒，西出阳关无故人。

Seeing Yuan the Second off to Anxi Protectorate [1]

The dust of Wei City was damped by the morning rain. [2]
The roadhouse is dark green and the willows are fresh.
I want you to have a thorough drink once again.
Outside the Sunny Gate there are no old friends. [3]

1. Anxi Protectorate（安西都护府）, or Protectorate General to Pacify the West, was a protectorate established by the Tang Dynasty in 640.
2. The Wei City（渭城）was also named Xianyang（咸阳）, it was the capital of Qin.
3. Sunny Gate, or Yangguan Pass（阳关）, lies to the south of Jade Gate, or Yumen Pass. They are two most important western passes. The Anxi Protectorate lay west of them.

鹿柴

空山不见人，但闻人语响。
返景入深林，复照青苔上。

Deer Enclosure [1]

Nobody can be seen in this empty mountain.
But voices are heard murmuring.
The light of sunset enters into the deep woods.
Then it falls on the green moss.

1. Deer Enclosure（鹿柴）was the name of a little place nearby Wang Wei's dwelling.

相思

红豆生南国，春来发几枝。
愿君多采撷，此物最相思。

Memory

In each spring of the South,
A few red beans come out.
Please pick off and take away,
They are the dearest memory.

栾家濑

飒飒秋雨中，浅浅石溜泻。
跳波自相溅，白鹭惊复下。

The Rapids of Luan Village

A pebbly stream rushes
In soughing autumn rain.
Mutually dash the splashes.
A stirred heron alights again.

白石滩

清浅白石滩，绿蒲向堪把。
家住水东西，浣纱明月下。

White Stone Shallows

The white stone shallows are clear,
The green water grass is so near.
Living somewhere beside the brook,
She washes the gauze under the moon.

竹里馆

独坐幽篁里，弹琴复长啸。
深林人不知，明月来相照。

A Dwelling in the Bamboos

Sitting in the quiet bamboos,
I play a zither and whistle high.
No one knows the deep woods,
Only the moon comes to shine.

山居秋暝

空山新雨后，天气晚来秋。
明月松间照，清泉石上流。
竹喧归浣女，莲动下渔舟。
随意春芳歇，王孙自可留。

The Mountain Life of An Autumn Evening

After a fresh rain in this empty mountain,
Comes the air of an autumn evening.
The bright moon shines through pines.
A clean stream flows over pebbles.
Swaying bamboos, some washer-girls come back.
Dividing lotuses, a fishing boat drifts down.
Let the fragrance of spring fade away.
But Your Highness could still stay.

田园乐

桃红复含宿雨，柳绿更带朝烟。
花落家童未扫，莺啼山客犹眠。

My Joyful Life in the Countryside

Holding raindrops of last night,
Peach flowers are red.
Enveloped by the morning mist,
Willow twigs are green.
Fallen petals are not swept
By the pupil of mine.
Singing birds cannot wake up
A man of mountain.

山中

荆溪白石出，天寒红叶稀。
山路元无雨，空翠湿人衣。

In the Mountains

White stones expose in the brambly river.
Red leaves decrease for the cold weather.
There is no rain over the mountain path.
It’s the moist air that damps the clothes.

山中送别

山中相送罢，日暮掩柴扉。
春草明年绿，王孙归不归？

A Parting in This Mountain

After a parting in this mountain,
I close the barrier at sunset.
Next spring the grass will green.
Would Your Highness come back?

酬张少府

晚年惟好静，万事不关心。
自顾无长策，空知返旧林。
松风吹解带，山月照弹琴。
君问穷通理，渔歌入浦深。

To Answer Minister Steward Zhang

When aged I only want to be quiet.
All those things I don’t care about.
I think I have nothing to advise,
But returning to the old woods.
The wind through pines blows my wear.
The moon above hills hears my zither.
You ask me the reason for rise and fall.
A fishing song from reeds answers now.

送别

下马饮君酒，问君何所之。
君言不得意，归卧南山陲。
但去莫复问，白云无尽时。

Farewell

You dismount to have a drink.
Then I ask the destination of you.
You tell me your disappointment,
And you'll desert in countryside.
Go ahead and do not waver.
White clouds float forever.

杂诗

君自故乡来，应知故乡事。
来日绮窗前，寒梅著花未？

A Sketch

From our hometown you have newly come.
News of hometown you should tell me some.
By the window before you left,
Had the winter-sweet bloomed?

鸟鸣涧

人闲桂花落，夜静春山空。
月出惊山鸟，时鸣春涧中。

Warbles in a Ravine

Sweet flowers are falling on an idle man.
Spring mountains were left for the quiet night.
Mountain birds are stirred by the rising moon.
They warble in a spring ravine from time to time.

渡荆门送别

渡远荆门外，来从楚国游。
山随平野尽，江入大荒流。
月下飞天镜，云生结海楼。
仍怜故乡水，万里送行舟。

Farewell After Passing Through the Jing Gate [1]

Having sailed far beyond the Jing Gate,
I come to travel over the Chu State.
The mountains fade into the plain,
And the river spreads to the vast.
The falling moon is a flying heavenly mirror,
While the rising clouds form a seaborne tower.
Still I cherish the water of my home.
For a long time it has been carrying my boat.

1. Jing Gate is a key pass between Shu and Chu.

望庐山瀑布

日照香炉生紫烟，遥看瀑布挂前川。
飞流直下三千尺，疑是银河落九天。

Watching the Cataract of Mount Lu [1]

Under the sunlight smokes the Censer Peak.
Far away I see the cataract hang as a curtain.
Waters fly down straight three thousand feet.
Does the Milky Way fall from the ninth heaven?

1. Mount Lu or Lushan（庐山）is situated in the northern part of Jiangxi Province in Central China, and is one of the most renowned mountains in the country.

望天门山

天门中断楚江开，碧水东流至此回。
两岸青山相对出，孤帆一片日边来。

Watching the Sky Gate Mountain

The Sky Gate is broken by the Chu River, [1]
Which hurries east but twists and turns here.
Green hills on both sides come out in twos.
A piece of sail beside the sun floats alone.

1. The Sky Gate Mountain（天门山）is in now Wuhu City（芜湖市）, Anhui Province. The Chu River is a section of Chang Jiang in ancient Chu State.

山中问答

问余何意栖碧山，笑而不答心自闲。
桃花流水窅然去，别有天地非人间。

A Dialogue in a Mountain

You ask me why I reside in this green mountain.
At leisure I answer you with no word but a grin.
Peach flowers were taken by water from the distance.
Where a new world without a worry is in existence.

静夜思

床前明月光，疑是地上霜。
举头望明月，低头思故乡。

Quiet Night Thought

The bright light before my bed,
Looks like frost on the ground.
Raising head I gaze on the moon.
Bowing head I think of my home.

黄鹤楼送孟浩然之广陵

故人西辞黄鹤楼，烟花三月下扬州。
孤帆远影碧空尽，唯见长江天际流。

Seeing Meng Haoran off to Guangling at the Yellow Crane Tower[1]

My dear friend has left the Yellow Crane Tower.
He boats down to Yangzhou in the flowery season.
The faraway and solitary sail fades into the blue air.
I can see only Chang Jiang flowing to the horizon.[2]

1. Guangling was a name of now Yangzhou（扬州）.
2. Chang Jiang means "long river" in Chinese language. It is the longest river of China and of Asia.

蜀道难

噫吁嚱，危乎高哉！
蜀道之难，难于上青天！
蚕丛及鱼凫，开国何茫然！
尔来四万八千岁，不与秦塞通人烟。
西当太白有鸟道，可以横绝峨眉巅。
地崩山摧壮士死，然后天梯石栈相钩连。

The Roads to Shu Are Hard [1]

Eek boo hoo! Too steep and too high!
It's harder to walk the Shu Roads than to ascend the sky!
Of founding kings from Silkworm to Osprey, [2]
Little can be known about the early history.
In the forty-eight thousand years following,
Shu had no come and go with Qin.
Beginning with Mount Taibai to the west, [3]
The way of birds leads straight to Mount Emei's crest. [4]
Not until the deaths of heroes in earthquakes and landslides,
Could precipice roads be linked with skyward ladders.

1. The Roads to Shu are mountain roads linking Shaanxi with Sichuan.
2. Silkworm and Osprey were two kings of ancient Shu.
3. Mount Taibai, or Mount Great White, is located in the southwest of Shaanxi Province. It is the dominant peak of Qin Mountains and the highest peak to the east of Qing-Zang Plateau.
4. Mount Emei sits at the western rim of the Sichuan Basin. It is the highest one of the Four Sacred Buddhist Mountains of China.

上有六龙回日之高标，下有冲波逆折之回川。
黄鹤之飞尚不得过，猿猱欲度愁攀援。
青泥何盘盘，百步九折萦岩峦。
扪参历井仰胁息，以手抚膺坐长叹。

A lofty mark on high reminds six dragons to drag back the sun.
A winding river at bottom forces waves to dash and run.
Yellow cranes fail to fly over.
Worried monkeys stop to climb up.
How convoluted are the roads of Mud Heights! [5]
In one hundred steps you should turn nine times.
Almost touching stars, you straighten up to inhale. [6]
Stroking your chest, you sit down to sigh.

5. The Mud Heights, or Qingni Heights（青泥岭）, are in now Hanzhong（汉中）, Shaanxi.
6. The stars in original text belong to two southwest mansions named Sen（参）and Jing（井）. These two mansions represent Shu and Qin separately.

问君西游何时还？畏途巉岩不可攀。
但见悲鸟号古木，雄飞雌从绕林间。
又闻子规啼夜月，愁空山。

When would you return from the westward travel?
Don’t climb those paths fearful and rocks terrible.
You could see woeful birds crying by an old tree,
A male and a female flying together in the woods.
You could hear a cuckoo sobbing under the moon,
And complaining the empty mountains.

蜀道之难，难于上青天，使人听此凋朱颜！
连峰去天不盈尺，枯松倒挂倚绝壁。
飞湍瀑流争喧豗，砯崖转石万壑雷。
其险也如此，嗟尔远道之人，胡为乎来哉！

It's harder to walk the Shu Roads than to ascend the sky!
These words change one's face into gray from red.
Clustered peaks part from the sky less than one foot.
Withered pines hang upside-down along the crag.
The turbulence and the falls compete their noise.
Cracked rocks and rolling stones thunder in ravines.
So dangerous they are!
Why on earth did you come here from afar?

剑阁峥嵘而崔嵬，一夫当关，万夫莫开。
所守或匪亲，化为狼与豺。
朝避猛虎，夕避长蛇。磨牙吮血，杀人如麻。
锦城虽云乐，不如早还家。
蜀道之难，难于上青天，侧身西望长咨嗟！

Mount Sword is pointy and the Gallery Roads are chancy. [7]
One man guards, ten thousand men can't pass.
If you encounter the unfamiliar watches,
They might change into greedy wolves.
All day and all night,
You should evade savage tigers and long snakes.
Having killed countless people,
They grind their teeth and suck people's blood.
Though the Brocade Official City is good, [8]
But going home early is better.
It's harder to walk the Shu Roads than to ascend the sky!
I look awry into the west distance and draw a deep sigh.

7. Jiange（剑阁）is in Sichuan Province. Its name derived from the Gallery Roads（阁道）in Mount Sword（剑山）. It is notable that the Gallery Roads consist of wooden planks erected on wooden or stone beams slotted into holes cut into the sides of cliffs.
8. "The Brocade Official City" is another name of Chengdu（成都）, which is the central city of Shu or Sichuan. The brocade of Shu, or Shujin（蜀锦）, is a special local product.

行路难

金樽清酒斗十千，玉盘珍羞直万钱。
停杯投箸不能食，拔剑四顾心茫然。
欲渡黄河冰塞川，将登太行雪满山。
闲来垂钓碧溪上，忽复乘舟梦日边。
行路难！行路难！多歧路，今安在？
长风破浪会有时，直挂云帆济沧海。

Roads Are Hard

The clean wine in gold cup needs a lot of money.
The delicious food on jade plate is very costly.
But I lay the cup aside and put chopsticks down.
Drawing out my sword I absently look around.
The Yellow River has been iced before my crossing.
The Taihang Mountains have been snowed before my ascending. [1]
Jiang Shang had angled on a green creek leisurely.
Yi Yin had dreamed of boating by the sun suddenly. [2]
Roads are hard! Roads are Hard!
So many branches, where you are?
Someday the cloud-like sails will be pushed by the long wind,
And the ship will cut through waves and arrive a distant land.

1. The Taihang Mountains（太行山）are the eastern edge of the Loess Plateau.
2. Jiang Shang（姜尚）helped Kings Wen and Wu of Zhou Dynasty overthrow Shang Dynasty. Yi Yin（伊尹）helped King Tang of Shang Dynasty overthrow Xia Dynasty. Here Li Bai told two stories of Jiang Shang and Yi Yin before their being appointed as prime minister.

山中与幽人对酌

两人对酌山花开，一杯一杯复一杯。
我醉欲眠卿且去，明朝有意抱琴来。

Drinking With a Hermit in a Mountain

When mountain flowers bloom we meet,
And drink one cup of wine after another.
I'm drunk and sleepy, you should leave.
Tomorrow you can come with a zither.

将进酒

君不见黄河之水天上来，奔流到海不复回。
君不见高堂明镜悲白发，朝如青丝暮成雪。
人生得意须尽欢，莫使金樽空对月。
天生我材必有用，千金散尽还复来。

Do Drink More

Don't you see that
The water of the Yellow River coming from the sky
And rushing into the sea
Is never back?
Don't you see that
The mirror of the Grand Hall reflecting black threads at dawn
But white snow at night
Is so sad? [1]
Do pursue pleasure when be in a cheerful mood.
Don't let the gold cup be empty under the moon.
Our talents given by Heaven are doomed to work.
Countless money being scattered will come back.

1. Being higher and wider, the Grand Hall in a traditional Chinese family courtyard is usually dwelt by the parents.

烹羊宰牛且为乐，会须一饮三百杯。
岑夫子，丹丘生，
将进酒，杯莫停。
与君歌一曲，请君为我倾耳听。
钟鼓馔玉不足贵，但愿长醉不愿醒。
古来圣贤皆寂寞，惟有饮者留其名。

Don’t hesitate to kill cattle and cook sheep.
Do drink hundreds of cups without a break.
Cen the senior, and Danqiu the junior [2],
Do drink more, and don’t stop.
I’ll sing a song for you,
Please lend an attentive ear to me.
Don’t stint the luxury orchestra and the delicate food.
Do indulge in a long intoxication and not to wake up.
Most sages in the past are forgotten.
But drinkers are often well-known.

2. Cen Xun（岑勋）and Yuan Danqiu（元丹丘）were friends of Li Bai.

陈王昔时宴平乐，斗酒十千恣欢谑。
主人何为言少钱，径须沽取对君酌。
五花马，千金裘，
呼儿将出换美酒，与尔同销万古愁。

The Prince Chen once dined at the Peace Joy Temple. [3]
The wine of ten thousand coins a cask was supplied at will.
Don't complaint of lacking money, you the host.
Do just buy more wine and let's drink together.
The rare horse and the dear fur,
Should be handed out and swapped for the fine liquor.
Let's have the sorrow of millenniums molten forever.

3. Prince Chen, or Cao Zhi (曹植) , was a prince of Wei kingdom in the Three Kingdoms period of China, and an outstanding poet. The Peace Joy Temple lay outside the west gate of Luoyang.

送友人

青山横北郭，白水绕东城。
此地一为别，孤蓬万里征。
浮云游子意，落日故人情。
挥手自兹去，萧萧班马鸣。

Seeing My Friend Off

Green hills lie before the north wall.
A white river circles the east city.
After we say bye here and now.
You will travel long and lonely.
A cloud has decided to set out.
The sun would rather sink slowly.
You wave your hand and turn around.
The neighs fade away and away.

客中作

兰陵美酒郁金香，玉碗盛来琥珀光。
但使主人能醉客，不知何处是他乡。

Being a Guest

The wine of Lanling has the scent of ginger.[1]
Bowls of jade are filled with lights of amber.
If a host could make a guest drink a lot,
The latter would forget whether he lives abroad.

1. Lanling（兰陵）is in southern Shandong Province.

子夜吴歌（秋歌）

长安一片月，万户捣衣声。
秋风吹不尽，总是玉关情。
何日平胡虏，良人罢远征？

Midnight Songs of Wu（The Autumn Song）[1]

Chang'an is covered by the moonlight.
Countless wives pound clothes tonight.
The autumn wind can't blow away
The long longing toward Jade Gate.
When will the barbarians be annihilated,
And the husbands in expedition be liberated?

1. Songs of Wu are folk songs of a region around Lake Tai. Li Bai wrote four songs for four seasons and this one was for the autumn.

清平调词三首

（一）

云想衣裳花想容，春风拂槛露华浓。

若非群玉山头见，会向瑶台月下逢。

Three Songs of the Clear Calm Melody [1]

I

The clouds look like her clothes and the flowers her face.
The spring wind strokes rails and the dewdrops are dense.
If it wasn't seen on the top of Assembled Jade Mountain,
It must happen under the moon of Concave Jade Space. [2]

1. It was said that these three poems were written under the order of Emperor Xuanzong when Xuanzong and Sub-Empress Yang（杨贵妃）enjoyed the tree peonies at Pavilion Immersed in Sweet.
2. According to *The Biography of Son of Heaven Mu*（《穆天子传》）, Queen Mother of the West（西王母）dwelt in the Piked Jades Mountain and met King Mu of Zhou Dynasty at the Concave Jade Space.

（二）

一枝红艳露凝香，云雨巫山枉断肠。
借问汉宫谁得似，可怜飞燕倚新妆。

II

A red and hot flower has her fragrance condensed into dew.
The clouds and rain of Mount Wu is unworthy of longing for. [3]
If you inquire who in the palace of Han Dynasty resembles her.
It's pitiful that even Flying Swallow should have to do makeup. [4]

3. The clouds and rain of Mount Wu（巫山） was governed by a Goddess. She was described by Song Yu（宋玉） for King Qingxiang of Chu（楚顷襄王）, then King Qingxiang longed for her.
4. Flying Swallow is paraphrased from Zhao Feiyan's personal name. Zhao Feiyan was an empress during the Han Dynasty. Her husband was Emperor Cheng（汉成帝）. She was often compared and contrasted with Sub-Empress Yang, because she was known for her slender build while Yang was known for her full build.

（三）

名花倾国两相欢，长得君王带笑看。

解释春风无限恨，沉香亭北倚阑干。

III

Both the notable flowers and the national beauty are pleasing.

All the time the Sovereign looks at her smiling.

Many sorrows of the spring wind are released,

Beside the north rails of a pavilion immersed in sweet.

月下独酌

花间一壶酒，独酌无相亲。
举杯邀明月，对影成三人。
月既不解饮，影徒随我身。
暂伴月将影，行乐须及春。
我歌月徘徊，我舞影凌乱。
醒时同交欢，醉后各分散。
永结无情游，相期邈云汉。

Drinking Alone Under the Moon

Among flowers lies a pot of wine.
I drink it without a friend of mine.
Rising wine I invite the bright moon,
And my shadow is the third person.
The moon cannot understand me.
The shadow can only imitate me.
Temporarily we three get together,
In the spring to pursue pleasure.
The moon wanders for my singing.
The shadow sways for my dancing.
We share joy when I'm awake.
We disperse when I fall asleep.
The moon is cold-hearted forever.
I date her beyond the stellar river.

戏赠杜甫

饭颗山头逢杜甫，顶戴笠子日卓午。
借问别来太瘦生，总为从前作诗苦。

A Joke With Du Fu [1]

On Mount Grain, I encounter Du Fu. [2]
He wears a bamboo hat at high noon.
"Than last time why do you look even thinner?"
"All the time, poem-writing is so bitter."

1. Li Bai is called the Immortal of Poem（诗仙）, and Du Fu is called the Saint of Poem（诗圣）. These two greatest poets were close friends.
2. Mount Grain was not a mountain, but a bowl of cooked grain Du Fu was eating.

梦游天姥吟留别

海客谈瀛洲，烟涛微茫信难求。
越人语天姥，云霞明灭或可睹。
天姥连天向天横，势拔五岳掩赤城。
天台四万八千丈，对此欲倒东南倾。

Ascending Mount Tianmu in a Dream [1]

Of Ying Island, sailors spoke: [2]
"It's hard to be confirmed on faraway and misty waves."
Of Mount Tianmu, Yue-men told: [3]
"It's possible to be seen amid white and red clouds.
Tianmu springs to and connects the Heaven.
It surpasses the Five Great Mountains and screens off Mount Chicheng. [4]
Mount Tiantai is four hundred and eighty thousand feet. [5]
Facing Tianmu it seems to evade southeast."

1. Mount Tianmu（天姥山）, or Mount Heavenly Grandma, is in Xinchang County（新昌县）, Shaoxing City（绍兴市）, Zhejiang Province.
2. Ying Island（瀛洲）is a mythological island where immortals live.
3. Yue was a state in now Zhejiang during the Spring and Autumn Period.
4. The Five Great Mountains or Wuyue（五岳）are arranged according to the five cardinal directions. They are Mount Tai（泰山）sitting in the east, Mount Hua（华山）standing in the west, Mount Heng（恒山）walking in the north, Mount Heng（衡山）flying in the south, and Mount Song（嵩山）lying in the center. Mount Chicheng（赤城山）, or Mount Red City Wall, has red rocks arraying like walls. It lie to the south of Mount Tiantai.
5. Mount Tiantai（天台山）, or Mount Heavenly Terrace, is a mountain in Tiantai County near the city of Taizhou（台州）, Zhejiang. Its highest peak, Huading（华顶）, reaches a height of 1138 meters.

我欲因之梦吴越，一夜飞渡镜湖月。
湖月照我影，送我至剡溪。
谢公宿处今尚在，渌水荡漾清猿啼。

So I dream of Wu and Yue.
And fly across Lake Mirror. [6]
The moon and my shadow accompany me
From the lake to the Shan Stream. [7]
A lodge of noble Xie is still there, [8]
And monkeys howl by the waving water.

6. Lake Mirror（鉴湖）lies to the southwest of Shaoxing City.
7. The Shan Stream（剡溪）is an upper section of the Cao'e River（曹娥江）.
8. Xie Lingyun（谢灵运）, was a poet of Southern Dynasties（南朝）.

脚著谢公屐，身登青云梯。
半壁见海日，空中闻天鸡。
千岩万转路不定，迷花倚石忽已暝。
熊咆龙吟殷岩泉，慄深林兮惊层巅。

Wearing Xie's clogs, [9]
I climb the ladder in clouds.
On the cliff I see the sea-sun arising.
In the air I hear the sky-cock crowing.
Thousands of blocking rocks make the path uncertain.
When I rest enjoying flowers, it gets dark all of a sudden.
Roars of bears and hums of dragons pervade waterfalls.
The deepest forest scares and the highest peak fears.

9. The clogs of Xie had adjustable shoe heels which set behind when ascending and set before when descending.

云青青兮欲雨，水澹澹兮生烟。
列缺霹雳，丘峦崩摧。
洞天石扉，訇然中开。
青冥浩荡不见底，日月照耀金银台。
霓为衣兮风为马，云之君兮纷纷而来下。
虎鼓瑟兮鸾回车，仙之人兮列如麻。

Getting black, the clouds would rain.
Looked uneasy, the pool is smoking.
A lightning and thunders,
Destroy rocks.
A stone gate of cavern,
Is banged open.
The bottom of an immense and profound space cannot be seen.
Gold and silver buildings here are shone by the sun and moon.
Wearing rainbow-clothes and riding wind-horses,
Men of cloud land descend one by one.
Tigers play musics and phoenixes drag carriages.
Countless immortals line up.

忽魂悸以魄动，怳惊起而长嗟。
惟觉时之枕席，失向来之烟霞。
世间行乐亦如此，古来万事东流水，别君去兮何时还？
且放白鹿青崖间，须行即骑访名山。
安能摧眉折腰事权贵，使我不得开心颜！

Suddenly my soul palpitates.
Then I wake up and draw a long sigh.
Have gone away all those glorious.
Only left are pillow and mat.
Earthly delights are just like this journey.
All things of old times have flowed away.
They left you and never had a stay.
My white deer is freed among green cliffs.
I'll ride it to a famous mountain when necessary.
Why should I bow and scrape to those lords,
And make myself feel unhappy?

古风（三）

秦王扫六合，虎视何雄哉！
挥剑决浮云，诸侯尽西来。
明断自天启，大略驾群才。
收兵铸金人，函谷正东开。

Archaism (III)

The King of Qin cleaned up the world.
So powerfully he watched like a tiger.
Trivial matters were ended by sword.
All other kings went west to surrender.
Wise decisions came from the Providence.
Many talents obeyed the great intelligence.
Into statues the confiscated weapons were cast.
To the east the Hangu Pass was opened just. [1]

1. Hangu Pass was the choke point shielding Qin from attacks of the eastern states.

铭功会稽岭，骋望琅琊台。
刑徒七十万，起土骊山隈。
尚采不死药，茫然使心哀。
连弩射海鱼，长鲸正崔嵬。

He had achievements inscribed on Mount Kuaiji. [2]
He rode the Langya tableland and looked around. [3]
Seven hundred thousand prisoners were gathered.
To build his mausoleum in the cove of Mount Li. [4]
He indulged in gaining the long-live medicine.
But his heart was broken for finding nothing.
Some creature in the sea was shoot incessantly.
A long whale came out and it was huge and lofty.

2. Mount Kuaiji was legendarily connected with Yu the Great（大禹）. After uniting China, Qin Shi Huang inscribed here to commemorate Yu the Great and publicize the achievements of his own.
3. Langya tableland is in now Qingdao City, Shandong Province. Qin Shi Huang came here three times.
4. Mount Li is a mountain located in the northeast of Xi'an in Shaanxi Province.

额鼻象五岳，扬波喷云雷。
鬐鬣蔽青天，何由睹蓬莱？
徐市载秦女，楼船几时回？
但见三泉下，金棺葬寒灰。

With a mountain-like nose and head,
It raised waves and sprayed thunderclouds.
Its dorsal fin screened off the blue sky.
How could be seen the Penglai Island? [5]
Xu Shi took away thousands of children. [6]
When would his majestic vessels return?
Under the third layer of groundwater,
Only the cold ash in the gold coffin is there.

5. Penglai is a legendary land of Chinese mythology. It is said to be on an island in the eastern end of Bohai Sea (渤海), along with four other islands where the immortals lived, called Fanghu (方壶), Yingzhou (瀛洲), Daiyu (岱舆), and Yuanqiao (员峤).
6. Xu Shi (徐市), or Xu Fu (徐福), was sent by Qin Shi Huang to the eastern seas twice to look for the long-live medicine. It was believed that the fleet included 60 barques and around 5000 crew members, 3000 boys and girls, and craftsmen of different fields. After he embarked on a second mission, he never returned.

战城南

去年战，桑干源；
今年战，葱河道。
洗兵条支海上波，放马天山雪中草。
万里长征战，三军尽衰老。

Fighting Near the South Inner City Wall [1]

Last year, we fought
At the source of the Sanggan River. [2]
This year, we fight
In a valley of the Scallion Ridges. [3]
Swords were washed by waves of the sea beside Tiaozhi. [4]
Horses were freed to grass in the snow on Tian Shan. [5]
Having fought thousands of miles,
All fighters are old and weak.

1. Fighting Near the South Inner City Wall once was a title of Yuefu（乐府）in Han Dynasty. Yuefu, or Music Bureau, was an governmental organization charged with collecting or writing the lyrics, later it was applied to literary imitations or adaptations of the Music Bureau's poems. Adopting this title, later poets may mean just"bloody battles".
2. The source of the Sanggan River is in the north of Shanxi Province.
3. The Scallion Ridges, or Congling（葱岭）, was an name of the Pamir Mountains from Han Dynasty on.
4. According to the reports of Zhang Qian（张骞）the envoy of Han Dynasty, Tiaozhi（条支）was the Seleucid Empire in Mesopotamia.
5. Tian Shan（天山）, meaning the Heavenly Mountains, is located in Central Asia.

匈奴以杀戮为耕作，古来惟见白骨黄沙田。
秦家筑城备胡处，汉家还有烽火燃。
烽火燃不息，征战无已时。

Huns regard killing as farming.
All along they plant white bones in yellow sands.
Upon forts built by Qin to defend,
Beacon fires were still lighted by Han.
Beacon fires never die out.
Fierce fights never stop.

野战格斗死，败马号鸣向天悲。
乌鸢啄人肠，衔飞上挂枯树枝。
士卒涂草莽，将军空尔为。
乃知兵者是凶器，圣人不得已而用之。

In field battles the fighters die.
Their wounded horses yell and cry toward the sky.
Crows and eagles peck the bowels,
Then take them away and hang them on dry branches.
Soldiers decay in the wilderness.
Only one general is worthless.
So we know that the warfare is too dangerous.
It's the last method for the Sage to use.

宣州谢朓楼饯别校书叔云

弃我去者，昨日之日不可留。
乱我心者，今日之日多烦忧。

A Farewell Dinner With My Uncle the Reviser Li Yun on the Tower of Xie Tiao in Xuanzhou [1]

Having left me, the day of yesterday went away.
Disturbing me, the day of today is full of worry.

1. Xie Tiao was a poet of Southern Qi and once was the governor of Xuanzhou（宣州）. He was called Junior Xie in comparison with the senior Xie Lingyun.

长风万里送秋雁，对此可以酣高楼。
蓬莱文章建安骨，中间小谢又清发。
俱怀逸兴壮思飞，欲上青天揽明月。

Autumn geese are being sent by the long wind.
It’s worth ascending a height to have a drink.
The literature had changed from fat to thin.
Then the Junior Xie was fresh and clean.
We chat so cheerfully that we want to fly,
And to embrace the moon high in the sky.

抽刀断水水更流，举杯消愁愁更愁。
人生在世不称意，明朝散发弄扁舟。

Cut by a sword, the water still flows.
Melted by the wine, the sorrow even grows.
Many past things of my life were unhappy.
Tomorrow I'll loosen my hair and float away.

独坐敬亭山

众鸟高飞尽，孤云独去闲。
相看两不厌，只有敬亭山。

Sitting Alone Before the Jingting Mountain [1]

All birds have flown high away.
A lonely cloud has left idly.
Can appreciate each other indeed,
Only the Jingting Mountain and me.

1. The Jingting Mountain is in now the Xuancheng City of Anhui Province.

哭晁卿衡

日本晁衡辞帝都，孤帆一片绕蓬壶。
明月不归沉碧海，白云愁色满苍梧。

Crying for Chao Heng [1]

The Japanese Chao Heng left the Imperial Capital.
A piece of sail winded through the rocks of east shoal.
Now the bright moon vanishes and lies beneath the blue sea.
The white clouds above the south seaside are full of grief.

1. Abe no Nakamaro（阿倍仲麻吕）, whose Chinese name was Chao Heng（晁衡）, was a Japanese envoy, scholar and poet. He moved to Tang Dynasty China in 717. In 752, he tried to return to Japan but the ship he was traveling in was wrecked and ran aground off the coast of Vietnam, but he managed to return to Chang'an in 755. He took several government offices and died in 770, chang'an. He was a close friend of Li Bai, who believed that he had died in the wreck.

秋浦歌十七首（其十四）

炉火照天地，红星乱紫烟。
赧郎明月夜，歌曲动寒川。

A Song of the Autumn Shores（The Fourteenth of Seventeen）[1]

The fire illuminates the earth and sky.
Red sparks scatter in purple smoke.
Blushers in the night with moonlight,
Sing songs shaking the cold river.

1. The Autumn Shores, or Qiupu（秋浦）, was a place producing silver and copper in Tang Dynasty. In this poem, Li Bai described the work of smelters.

秋浦歌十七首（其十五）

白发三千丈，缘愁似个长。
不知明镜里，何处得秋霜。

A Song of the Autumn Shores (The Fifteenth of Seventeen) [1]

The length of my white hair is thirty thousand feet,
And the sorrow of mine is as long as it.
Where does my mirror get from,
The frost of autumn?

1. Li Bai wrote this poem in his fifties.

赠汪伦

李白乘舟将欲行，忽闻岸上踏歌声。
桃花潭水深千尺，不及汪伦送我情。

To Wang Lun

Li Bai gets on a boat and is about to leave.
Suddenly, he hears the tramp and chant on shore.
The depth of Peach Flowers Pool is a thousand feet.
But it's inferior to the feeling of Wang who sees me off.

早发白帝城

朝辞白帝彩云间，千里江陵一日还。
两岸猿声啼不住，轻舟已过万重山。

Leaving the Baidi City in the Early Morning [1]

At sunrise, I've left Baidi among the colorful clouds.
Today, I'd reach Jiangling after going hundreds of miles. [2]
Howls of monkeys constantly come from both sides.
My light boat has passed through thousands of hills.

1. Baidicheng or Baidi City is an ancient temple complex on a hill on the northern shore of Chang Jiang.
2. Jiangling, a historical name of Jingzhou, Hubei, China.

陪族叔刑部侍郎晔及中书贾舍人至游洞庭

南湖秋水夜无烟，耐可乘流直上天。
且就洞庭赊月色？将船买酒白云边。

Sailing on the Dongting Lake With My Uncle Ye the Assistant Minister of Justice and Jia the Secretary of General Office

The autumn water of south lake is bright in the night.
It seems that we could flow straight to the sky.
Temporarily borrowing from Dongting the moonlight,
We'll approach the white clouds to buy some wine.

哭宣城善酿纪叟

纪叟黄泉里，还应酿老春。
夜台无李白，沽酒与何人？

Crying for Ji the Old Brewer of Xuan Town

In the underworld, the old Ji
Must still brew mellow wine.
During the night, without Li
Whoever would come to buy?

崔颢

Cui Hao

黄鹤楼

昔人已乘黄鹤去，此地空余黄鹤楼。
黄鹤一去不复返，白云千载空悠悠。
晴川历历汉阳树，芳草萋萋鹦鹉洲。
日暮乡关何处是？烟波江上使人愁。

Yellow Crane Tower

Someone has flown away by a yellow crane.
Here the Yellow Crane Tower is left in vain.
The yellow crane has gone and will not reappear.
The white clouds have idled for a thousand years.
Trees are reflected in the shining Han River.
The Parrot Isle is covered with the aromatic herbs.
Looking at the setting sun, I long for my home.
Floating with a tiny boat, I fall into my woe.

凉州词

王翰

Wang Han

葡萄美酒夜光杯，欲饮琵琶马上催。
醉卧沙场君莫笑，古来征战几人回。

A Song of Liangzhou

The grape wine is fine, and the goblet is shining at night.
I want to have a drink, but a lute is urging us to ride.
Please don't laugh if I were dead drunk on battleground.
Since ancient times, few people have returned from fight.

张旭

Zhang Xu

山行留客

山光物态弄春晖，莫为轻阴便拟归。
纵使晴明无雨色，入云深处亦沾衣。

Wanting You to Keep on Mountaineering

All things in the mountains enjoy the spring light.
It seems a little rainy, but you don't have to return.
Even if the weather is completely sunny and bright.
In deep clouds, the clothes would be dampened.

次北固山下

客路青山外，行舟绿水前。
潮平两岸阔，风正一帆悬。
海日生残夜，江春入旧年。
乡书何处达？归雁洛阳边。

Approaching the Foot of Northern Firm Mountain

Roads wind through the blue mountains.
My boat advances before the green waters.
The high tide makes the river wide.
The right wind pulls the sail tight.
In the remaining night, a sun from the sea rises.
Into the old year, a spring following the river enters.
Where would my letter home arrive?
For Luoyang, a goose has set off.

高适
Gao Shi

别董大

千里黄云白日曛，北风吹雁雪纷纷。
莫愁前路无知己，天下谁人不识君？

Seeing Dong the First Off

The yellow clouds spread a thousand miles, and the white sun is dusky.
The north wind blows wild geese, and the snowflakes flurry.
Don’t worry that there are no friends on your future way.
Whoever under the sky hasn’t heard of your fame?

储光羲

Chu Guangxi

钓鱼湾

垂钓绿湾春，春深杏花乱。
潭清疑水浅，荷动知鱼散。
日暮待情人，维舟绿杨岸。

An Angling Bay

I angle at a green bay in late spring,
When apricots in blossom are dazzling.
The clean pool appears to be not deep.
A moving lotus reveals where fishes were.
Waiting for my lover till eventide,
I tie my boat to a tree on the riverside.

逢雪宿芙蓉山主人

日暮苍山远，天寒白屋贫。
柴门闻犬吠，风雪夜归人。

Lodging in Mount Lotus to Avoid the Snow

The sun is low and the blue mountains are distant.
The air is cold and the white hut is destitute.
A dog barks beside the brush-wood gate.
A man returns in the snow-stormy night.

听弹琴

泠泠七弦上，静听松风寒。
古调虽自爱，今人多不弹。

Listening to the Zither

From seven clear strings,
Rises the cool wind of pine.
The old tune curing my feelings,
Is seldom played at the present time.

望岳

岱宗夫如何？齐鲁青未了。
造化钟神秀，阴阳割昏晓。
荡胸生层云，决眦入归鸟。
会当凌绝顶，一览众山小。

Mount Tai

How about Mount Tai?
It can be seen beyond Qi and Lu. [1]
Nature assembles all her best.
The ridge divides day and night.
Rising clouds sweep through my chest.
Return birds enter into my sight.
When I stand and watch on the crest,
All other mountains would become slight.

1. Mount Tai divided the ancient states Qi and Lu.

赠李白

秋来相顾尚飘蓬，未就丹砂愧葛洪。
痛饮狂歌空度日，飞扬跋扈为谁雄？

To Li Bai

We meet again in the autumn when you are still a drifter.
And you feel sorry to Ge Hong for failing to make an elixir. [1]
On dead drinking and mad singing your time was spent.
On what did your arrogance and arbitrariness depend?

1. Taoist Ge was Ge Hong of Eastern Jin Dynasty.

春日忆李白

白也诗无敌，飘然思不群。
清新庾开府，俊逸鲍参军。
渭北春天树，江东日暮云。
何时一樽酒，重与细论文？

Thinking of Li Bai in a Spring Day

Li Bai is unmatched in poetry writing.
Floating ideas of his are outstanding.
He's as fresh and clean as General Yu,
And as pretty and easy as Adviser Bao. [1]
A spring tree stands to the north of Wei River.
A sunset cloud tours to the east of Chang Jiang. [2]
When with wine would we get together,
Carefully again to discuss the literature?

1. General Yu, or Yu Xin（庾信）, and Adviser Bao, or Bao Zhao（鲍照）, were poets of the Southern and Northern Dynasties.
2. At that time, Du Fu was living to the north of Wei River and Li Bai to the east of Chang Jiang. Wei River is the biggest branch of the Yellow River.

饮中八仙歌

知章骑马似乘船，眼花落井水底眠。
汝阳三斗始朝天，道逢曲车口流涎，恨不移封向酒泉。
左相日兴费万钱，饮如长鲸吸百川，衔杯乐圣称避贤。
宗之潇洒美少年，举觞白眼望青天，皎如玉树临风前。

Eight Divine Drinkers

He Zhizhang, whose riding looks like sailing. [1]
He once fell in a well and sat in the water sleeping.
The King of Ruyang drinks at least three buckets one time. [2]
He salivated when a vehicle with distillers'grains went by.
He even wants his fief being shifted to Fountain of Wine. [3]
Left Premier, whose every banquet is sumptuous. [4]
He drinks like a huge whale sucking all streams,
And excuses his booze for yielding to the talents.
Cui Zongzhi, a graceful handsome young guy,
Raising his cup and rolling his eyes to the sky,
Is so bright like a jade tree with a breeze passing by.

1. He Zhizhang was the eldest of eight divine drinkers.
2. The King of Ruyang（汝阳王）was Li Jin（李琎）, a nephew of Emperor Xuanzong.
3. The Fountain of Wine or Jiuquan（酒泉）, is in now Gansu Province.
4. The Left Premier was Li Shizhi（李适之）.

苏晋长斋绣佛前，醉中往往爱逃禅。
李白一斗诗百篇，长安市上酒家眠，天子呼来不上船，自称臣是酒中仙。
张旭三杯草圣传，脱帽露顶王公前，挥毫落纸如云烟。
焦遂五斗方卓然，高谈雄辩惊四筵。

Su Jin always fasts before the portrait of Buddha,
Being drunk he often changes into a silent thinker.
Li Bai produces one hundred poems after drinking one bucket.
He once slept in a wine shop of Chang'an's market,
And nearly couldn't respond to the Emperor's invitation,
Saying "Your servant was a drunkard from Heaven".
Zhang Xu is blessed at cursive script after drinking a little.[5]
Taking off his hat and exposing his head before the nobles,
he put the clouds and smokes by a brush into a paper at will.
Jiao Sui would stand out after drinking five buckets.
His eloquent high voice startled all the people in banquet.

5. Zhang Xu was not only a poet but also a calligrapher, especially in cursive script.

出塞

挽弓当挽强，用箭当用长。
射人先射马，擒贼先擒王。
杀人亦有限，列国自有疆。
苟能制侵陵，岂在多杀伤？

Marching Out

Draw a strong bow.
Put a long arrow.
Shoot the rider’s horse.
Catch the foes’head.
Don’t kill too many.
Don’t chase too deep.
Were invaders confined,
Why not stop the fight?

春望

国破山河在，城春草木深。
感时花溅泪，恨别鸟惊心。
烽火连三月，家书抵万金。
白头搔更短，浑欲不胜簪。

Spring Sights

The state has been broken but the land remains. [1]
The city is in spring and the plants are dense.
Weeping at flowers, I think of the situation.
Startled by birds, I regret for the separation.
The warfare is continuous
And a letter from home is precious.
My white hair is scratched too thin
To be held by a hairpin.

1. In A.D.756, the rebel army of An Lushan（安禄山）took Chang'an.

石壕吏

暮投石壕村，有吏夜捉人。
老翁逾墙走，老妇出门看。
吏呼一何怒！妇啼一何苦！
听妇前致词：三男邺城戍。
一男附书至，二男新战死。
存者且偷生，死者长已矣。

A Minor Official at the Stony Trench Hamlet

At dusk I lodged in the hamlet Stony Trench,
At night somebody an official wanted to catch.
An old man climbed over the wall to flee,
An old woman opened the door to see.
How angrily the official yelled!
How painfully the woman wailed!
I heard the woman's words clearly:
"All my three sons has gone to defend Ye City.
One of them sent home a letter,
His two brothers had just died.
The left one is temporarily living,
The dead two are forever missing.

室中更无人，惟有乳下孙。
有孙母未去，出入无完裙。
老妪力虽衰，请从吏夜归。
急应河阳役，犹得备晨炊。
夜久语声绝，如闻泣幽咽。
天明登前途，独与老翁别。

There is no more man at home,
Only a grandson who clings to its Mum.
She can’t leave because of her child,
And she even has no wear to go out.
Though I’m old and frail,
Please take me right away.
Hastening to the north front,
I may timely do the breakfast.”
In the long silent night following,
Someone was heard sobbing.
At dawn I got on my own way,
Saying bye to the old man only.

蜀相

丞相祠堂何处寻，锦官城外柏森森。
映阶碧草自春色，隔叶黄鹂空好音。
三顾频烦天下计，两朝开济老臣心。
出师未捷身先死，长使英雄泪满襟。

The Premier of Shu [1]

Where can be found, the shrine of Premier?
Outside the Brocade City, it's in dense cypress woods.
Reflecting stairs, green grasses are in spring color.
Shaded by leaves, yellow birds make good sounds.
Being visited three times, you fetched out your grand strategy.
Assisting two generations, you devoted an old minister's heart.
Without the final win, you died of illness in the military camp.
Forever and ever, you will make heroes to weep tears.

1. The premier of Shu was Zhuge Liang (诸葛亮), a politician, military strategist, writer, engineer and inventor. He served as the premier of Han state in Shu during the Three Kingdoms period.

江村

清江一曲抱村流，长夏江村事事幽。
自去自来梁上燕，相亲相近水中鸥。
老妻画纸为棋局，稚子敲针作钓钩。
但有故人供禄米，微躯此外更何求？

A Riverside Village

A village is surrounded by a curve of clean river.
The riverside village has a long peaceful summer.
Swallows come from and go to the beam in singles.
Egrets get together and float on the water in doubles.
My old wife draws a paper into a chess board.
My little child knocks a needle into a fishhook.
So long as my friend has official rice to provide.
The negligible me has nothing else to require.

春夜喜雨

好雨知时节，当春乃发生。
随风潜入夜，润物细无声。
野径云俱黑，江船火独明。
晓看红湿处，花重锦官城。

A Nice Rain During a Spring Night

A nice rain is a wise rain.
It springs when it is spring.
Blown into night secretly,
It moistens things silently.
The clouds above wild paths are all black.
A lamp in riverboat is solely bright.
Tomorrow morning in the Brocade City,
Red and wet flowers will be heavy.

赠花卿

锦城丝管日纷纷，半入江风半入云。
此曲只应天上有，人间能得几回闻。

To Mr. Hua

Strings and pipes are played daily in the Silk Town.[1]
Some sounds go with the wind, some into the cloud.
Such music should belong only to the heaven.
People on the earth have little chance to listen.

1. Silk Town, or Brocade City, is now Chengdu.

不见

不见李生久，佯狂真可哀。
世人皆欲杀，吾意独怜才。
敏捷诗千首，飘零酒一杯。
匡山读书处，头白好归来。

Not Seen

I've not seen Li Bai for a long time.
It's so sad that he pretends to be mad.
People all want to put him to death.
I only remind that his talent is rare.
Hundreds of poems are written swift.
A cup of wine is drunk on the drift.
He once read books in Mount Kuang.[1]
When old he'd better come around.

1. Mount Kuang is in Shu, where Du Fu was living in then. He wanted Li Bai to come here again.

戏为六绝句（其二）

王杨卢骆当时体，轻薄为文哂未休。
尔曹身与名俱灭，不废江河万古流。

A Playful Quatrain（The Second of Six）

Wang, Yang, Lu and Luo created a new style. [1]
But frivolous writers sneered at it all the time.
Names of them had perished with their bodies.
While great rivers will flow for hundreds of centuries.

1. Wang, Yang, Lu and Luo are Wang Bo, Yang Jiong, Lu Zhaolin and Luo Binwang, they are praised as the Four Literary Eminences in Early Tang.

绝句二首（其二）

江碧鸟逾白，山青花欲燃。
今春看又过，何日是归年？

A Quatrain（The Second of Two）

Birds are even white against this green river.
Flowers look like fire on that blue mountain.
Clearly the spring of this year will be over.
To my hometown on which day can I return?

绝句四首（其三）

两个黄鹂鸣翠柳，一行白鹭上青天。
窗含西岭千秋雪，门泊东吴万里船。

A Quatrain (The Third of Four)

A pair of yellow birds chat on a green willow.
A line of white herons fly into the blue air.
The snow on west ridges is within my window.
The boats from east sea anchor outside my door.

旅夜书怀

细草微风岸，危樯独夜舟。
星垂平野阔，月涌大江流。
名岂文章著，官应老病休。
飘飘何所似？天地一沙鸥。

A Floater's Thought at Night

The kind breeze blows the fine grass.
A tall mast stands in the lonely night.
Above the broad and flat land hang stars.
In the big and flowing river sways moonlight.
How could the fame be achieved by a writer?
The office should be removed for my health.
What dose the floating me look like?
A sand bird between the sky and earth.

登高

风急天高猿啸哀，渚清沙白鸟飞回。
无边落木萧萧下，不尽长江滚滚来。
万里悲秋常作客，百年多病独登台。
艰难苦恨繁霜鬓，潦倒新停浊酒杯。

On the Height

Monkeys’howls go by the strong wind and rise into the high sky.
Fluttering birds hover above a clean islet and land on the white sands.
Leaves of innumerable plants fall and fall off.
Waves of the unceasing long river roll and roll in.
Far away from my home, I’ve grieved for many autumns.
Being alone on the height, I’m burdened with lots of illness.
Painstaking and distressed things make my hair even gray.
And recently, wine has been denied from my tedious life.

夜归

夜来归来冲虎过，山黑家中已眠卧。
傍见北斗向江低，仰看明星当空大。
庭前把烛嗔两炬，峡口惊猿闻一个。
白头老罢舞复歌，杖藜不睡谁能那？

Coming Back at Night

He comes back at night after rushing by a tiger.
His family has fallen asleep in this dark mountain.
Looking awry, he sees the Dipper hanging down to the river.
Looking up, he sees the Bright Star being big in the Heaven.
He scolds that two candles burn at the hall.
One startled ape responds beside the gorge.
The white-haired sings and waves a stick.
No one can persuade him to go to sleep.

江南逢李龟年

岐王宅里寻常见，崔九堂前几度闻。
正是江南好风景，落花时节又逢君。

Coming Across Li Guinian in the South [1]

Usually in Prince Qi's residence, sometimes at Courtier Cui's hall,
I've seen you and listened to your musical performance.
What a fine season of the South when flowers begin to fall.
I come across you again under this circumstance.

1. Li Guinian was a musician. Many years after An Lushan Rebellion, Du Fu came across him again.

白雪歌送武判官归京

岑参
Cen Shen

北风卷地白草折，胡天八月即飞雪。
忽如一夜春风来，千树万树梨花开。
散入珠帘湿罗幕，狐裘不暖锦衾薄。
将军角弓不得控，都护铁衣冷难着。

A Song of Snow: Seeing Military Judge off to the Capital

The north wind scrapes the land and crushes all plants.
Snowflakes fly under the alien sky early in the eighth month.
It looks as if the spring wind suddenly came at night,
And pear trees here and there were all in blossom.
They pass through bead curtains and wet gauze screens.
Fur coats are no longer warm and brocade quilts seem thin.
The horn-shaped bow of Commander is hard to draw.
The iron-made armor of Protector is too cold to wear.

瀚海阑干百丈冰，愁云惨淡万里凝。

Far-reaching ice walls crisscross on the vast sea.
Downcast stiff clouds screen off the greater light.

中军置酒饮归客，胡琴琵琶与羌笛。
纷纷暮雪下辕门，风掣红旗冻不翻。
轮台东门送君去，去时雪满天山路。
山回路转不见君，雪上空留马行处。

A banquet is held in headquarters for the returner.
Strings are touched or bowed and flutes are blown.
It snows heavily in the afternoon and we come out.
Red flags are too frozen to be turned over by the wind.
We see you off at the east gate of the Luntai fort. [1]
When the snow has fully covered the Tianshan's road.
The mountain road turns and we can't see you.
Only hoof-prints are left on the snow.

1. Luntai lies south to the Tianshan in Xinjiang Province.

逢入京使

故园东望路漫漫，双袖龙钟泪不干。
马上相逢无纸笔，凭君传语报平安。

Encountering a Messenger Sent to the Capital

Looking east towards my home, I see only the long road.
My sleeves are damp, but my tears still drop.
When riding we encounter, I have no ink or paper.
Please inform my family: I'm right in safety.

春怨

刘方平

Liu Fangping

纱窗日落渐黄昏，金屋无人见泪痕。
寂寞空庭春欲晚，梨花满地不开门。

Spring Sorrow

Outside the screen window,
There’s the sunset yellow.
Inside the golden boudoir,
No one witness your tear.
A pear tree is locked
In the lonely empty court.
Her petals are falling
In the dusk of late spring.

枫桥夜泊

月落乌啼霜满天，江枫渔火对愁眠。
姑苏城外寒山寺，夜半钟声到客船。

Mooring by a Bridge in a Windy Night

The moon is lost. The Crows cry out. The air becomes cold.
Riverside trees wave. Fishing lights wink. A sleepless man tosses about.
From the Cold Mountain Temple outside the Gusu Town,
Come the midnight tolls to my boat.

柏林寺南望

溪上遥闻精舍钟，泊舟微径度深松。
青山霁后云犹在，画出东南四五峰。

Looking Toward the Southwest From the Pinewoods Temple

On creek I hear the distant tolls of a preaching site.
So I moor my boat and hike through the woods of pine.
A rain has left the blue mountains but the clouds linger about.
Four or five peaks in the southeast are being painted out.

司空曙
Sikong Shu

江村即事

钓罢归来不系船，江村月落正堪眠。
纵然一夜风吹去，只在芦花浅水边。

An Occurrence in a Riverside Village

I let my boat untied after coming back from angling.
The moon of village has fallen, and it's time for sleeping.
Even if my boat was taken away by the wind at night.
It would still lie in the flowery reeds of riverside.

于良史

Yu Liangshi

春山夜月

春山多胜事，赏玩夜忘归。
掬水月在手，弄花香满衣。
兴来无远近，欲去惜芳菲。
南望鸣钟处，楼台深翠微。

The Spring Mountains in Moonlight Night

In the spring mountains, there are many sights.
I forget to return and linger into the night.
Holding some water, I get a moon in my hands.
Fondling flowers, I gain sweet on my dress.
If I want, I don't care about the distance.
Have to go! I do feel some reluctance.
Looking south at where the tolls come from,
I see buildings shaded by green and blue.

滁州西涧

独怜幽草涧边生，上有黄鹂深树鸣。
春潮带雨晚来急，野渡无人舟自横。

The West Stream of Chuzhou [1]

I like the quiet grass growing beside the stream,
And tweeting birds shaded by leaves of trees.
At dusk, a rain with floodwaters comes suddenly,
And an empty boat sways alone at the wild ferry.

1. Wei Yingwu once was the local official of Chuzhou in now the Anhui Province.

塞下曲六首（其二）

卢纶

Lu Lun

林暗草惊风，将军夜引弓。
平明寻白羽，没在石棱中。

A Border Song（The Second of Six）[1]

The grass in dark woods was startled by a blow.
It was a shoot from general Li at dusk.
The next dawn, they looked for the white plume of arrow.
It had been inserted into a corner of rock.

1. This poem was about a general in Han Dynasty named Li Guang who had shot a rock looked like a tiger.

塞下曲六首（其三）

月黑雁飞高，单于夜遁逃。
欲将轻骑逐，大雪满弓刀。

A Border Song（The Third of Six）

The moon hides and geese leave.
Fled the enemy chief.
Our cavalry is ready.
But the snow on armors is heavy.

喜见外弟又言别

李益

Li Yi

十年离乱后，长大一相逢。
问姓惊初见，称名忆旧容。
别来沧海事，语罢暮天钟。
明日巴陵道，秋山又几重。

I Meet My Cousin Happily，But We Have to Part Again

After parting in unrest, two adults encounter ten years later.
Before learning your full name, I mistakenly see you as a stranger.
An ocean of things we talk about, until the tolls of dusk ring out.
You have to leave tomorrow, and embark on the autumn mountain road.

写情

水纹珍簟思悠悠，千里佳期一夕休。
从此无心爱良夜，任他明月下西楼。

About Love

Lying on a ripple-figured mat, she longs for him,
But the engagement after a long wait is wiped out.
Hence she no longer cares about the good night,
And lets the bright moon get down from the tower.

孟郊

Meng Jiao

游子吟

慈母手中线，游子身上衣。
临行密密缝，意恐迟迟归。
谁言寸草心，报得三春晖！

A Song of a Traveling Son

The threads in the hands of my mother
Become the clothes of me the traveler.
Before my leaving, she sews carefully.
And the delay of my return is her worry.
If the tiny grass really wants.
Could it repay the spring warmth?

登科后

昔日龌龊不足夸，今朝放荡思无涯。
春风得意马蹄疾，一日看尽长安花。

A Winner in the Imperial Examination

Once the puny me could boast nothing.
Now I dare to think about everything.
In the pleasing wind of spring I ride quickly.
All the flowers in Chang'an are viewed in one day.

题都城南庄

崔护
Cui Hu

去年今日此门中，人面桃花相映红。
人面不知何处去，桃花依旧笑春风。

Dedicating to the South Road of Capital

On this day at last year and inside this gate,
I saw among pink flowers a pink face.
No one knows where the pink face has gone.
Only the flowers smile in the wind as before.

常建
Chang Jian

题破山寺后禅院

清晨入古寺，初日照高林。
曲径通幽处，禅房花木深。
山光悦鸟性，潭影空人心。
万籁此俱寂，但余钟磬音。

Dedicating to the Backyard of Broken Mountain Temple

I enter the old temple early in the morning.
Above high trees a newborn sun is shining.
A winding track leads to a secluded home.
In flowery plants lies a meditation abode.
Lights in the mountains coincide birds'nature.
Reflections in a pond empty my conjectures.
Millions of pipes quiet down at the moment.
Only left are tolls and knocks of instruments.

猛虎行

南山北山树冥冥，猛虎白日绕林行。
向晚一身当道食，山中麋鹿尽无声。
年年养子在深谷，雌雄上下不相逐。
谷中近窟有山村，长向村家取黄犊。
五陵年少不敢射，空来林下看行迹。

A Ferocious Tiger

The south and north mountains are covered with trees.
A ferocious tiger hovers here under the sunlight.
At dawn, she may eat alone and blocked the road.
All kinds of deer in the mountains are silent.
She breeds in this deep valley year after year.
Young males and females fallow in order.
There is a village in the valley near their cave.
Calves of villagers are often taken away.
The aristocratic youth approach the woods.
They detect the tracks but dare not shoot.

节妇吟

君知妾有夫，赠妾双明珠。
感君缠绵意，系在红罗襦。
妾家高楼连苑起，良人执戟明光里。
知君用心如日月，事夫誓拟同生死。
还君明珠双泪垂，恨不相逢未嫁时。

The Reply of a Chaste Wife

You've known that I'm a wife.
But you gave me pearls in pair.
Thanks for your long kindness,
I tied them to my red underwear.
The surrounding walls of my mansion are so high.
And my husband just stands there holding a pike.
Like the sun and moon, you care about me.
But whether live or die, I do belong to him.
With tears, I send your two pearls back.
For meeting too late, we can only sigh.

新嫁娘词

王建

Wang Jian

三日入厨下，洗手作羹汤。
未谙姑食性，先遣小姑尝。

Newly Married

She enters the kitchen three days later,
And washes her hands to make a soup.
Not knowing his mother's taste,
She invites his sister to savor.

雨过山村

雨里鸡鸣一两家，竹溪村路板桥斜。
妇姑相唤浴蚕去，闲着中庭栀子花。

After a Rain in a Mountain Village

When it still rains, one or two cocks crow.
At a crude bridge, a stream meets a road.
To wash cocoons, his wife and mother agree.
In the courtyard, a gardenia is left free.

左迁至蓝关示侄孙湘

一封朝奏九重天，夕贬潮州路八千。
欲为圣明除弊事，肯将衰朽惜残年！
云横秦岭家何在？雪拥蓝关马不前。
知汝远来应有意，好收吾骨瘴江边。

Words to My Grandnephew Xiang at Lan'guan on My Relegated Way [1]

At dawn, I raised a suggestion to the high top.
At night, I was relegated to Chaozhou far off.
I want to get rid of the wrongs for the Sage.
So I don't care of my feeble and frail age.
The long clouds of Qinling screen my home.
The heavy snow on Lan'guan blocks my horse.
I know why you travel so far to accompany me.
By the poisonous river you'll coffin my body.

1. Because of criticizing Buddhism, Han Yu was banished from Chang'an and appointed governor of Chaozhou in now the Guangdong Province. His Grandnephew Han Xiang met him at Lan'guan and would accompany him to Chaozhou. Lan'guan means blue pass, it lies southeast to Chang'an and north to Qingling which is a mountain range.

刘禹锡
Liu Yuxi

秋词

自古逢秋悲寂寥，我言秋日胜春朝。
晴空一鹤排云上，便引诗情到碧霄。

The Autumn

People all feel sad for the bleakness of autumn.
But I say that the autumn is better than the spring.
When a crane flies through the white clouds,
My poetic passion will be drawn into the blue sky.

赋得古原草送别

白居易

Bai Juyi

离离原上草，一岁一枯荣。
野火烧不尽，春风吹又生。
远芳侵古道，晴翠接荒城。
又送王孙去，萋萋满别情。

A Farewell Poem of Grass on the Antique Plain

The dried grass upon the plain,
Is coming alive once again.
Having been burned by wildfires,
It regrows in the spring air.
An old road is nearly buried,
And a solitary town is shaded.
I bid farewell to Your Highness.
The grassland is full of sadness.

夜雪

已讶衾枕冷，复见窗户明。
夜深知雪重，时闻折竹声。

Night Snow

Surprised by the bedding's cold,
I see the window paper turn bright.
Cracks of bamboos let me know:
The snow is heavy in the night.

大林寺桃花

人间四月芳菲尽，山寺桃花始盛开。
长恨春归无觅处，不知转入此中来。

Peach Flowers of the Great Woods Temple

Fragrance has melted away
In the fourth month of the lower world.
But peach flowers begin to bloom
In this mountain temple.
I often complained that the past spring
Is nowhere to be found.
Now I realize that it has moved up
And enter into this ground.

问刘十九

绿蚁新醅酒，红泥小火炉。
晚来天欲雪，能饮一杯无？

Ask Liu XIX

The unfiltered new wine looks green.
A little clayey stove has turned red.
The snow would come with the night.
Could you have a drink with me?

暮江吟

一道残阳铺水中，半江瑟瑟半江红。
可怜九月初三夜，露似真珠月似弓。

The River at Dusk

A long fragmentary sun spreads over the water,
Which is red on one half and raw on the other.
The third night of the ninth month is a little cold.
Dewdrops look like pearls and the moon a bow.

李绅

Li Shen

悯农二首（其一）

春种一粒粟，秋收万颗子。
四海无闲田，农夫犹饿死。

A Pitiful Peasant（The First of Two）

Sow a seed in spring.
Gain a lot in autumn.
No field is idling.
Peasants still starve.

悯农二首（其二）

锄禾日当午，汗滴禾下土。
谁知盘中餐，粒粒皆辛苦。

A Pitiful Peasant（The Second of Two）

Hoe till the noon.
Sweat wets the soil.
Each grain you eat,
Comes from labor.

柳宗元
Liu Zongyuan

江雪

千山鸟飞绝，万径人踪灭。
孤舟蓑笠翁，独钓寒江雪。

Snowy River

Hundreds of hills, no bird.
Thousands of paths, no walker.
On a boat, in a cape, under a hat,
Angling among snowflakes, a man old.

闻乐天授江州司马

元稹
Yuan Zhen

残灯无焰影幢幢，此夕闻君谪九江。
垂死病中惊坐起，暗风吹雨入寒窗。

Hearing That Letian Has Been Relegated as Assistant to Jiangzhou [1]

Shadows sway and the light is about to die out.
Hearing that you've been relegated to Jiangzhou,
I'm stirred from the deadly illness to sit up.
The rain is secretly blown into the cold window.

1. Letian was another name of Bai Juyi, who was a confidant of Yuan Zhen.

离思

曾经沧海难为水，除却巫山不是云。
取次花丛懒回顾，半缘修道半缘君。

Without You [1]

After reaching the Wu Mountains and the far ocean,
To the common waters and clouds I pay no attention.
Walking through flowers I have no desire to review.
It is due half to the Tao-practice and half to you.

1. A poem written for his dead wife.

剑客

贾岛
Jia Dao

十年磨一剑，霜刃未曾试。
今日把示君，谁有不平事？

Swordsman

Ten years to whet.
The thin never tried.
Today I show it.
Tell me the unjust.

题李凝幽居

闲居少邻并，草径入荒园。
鸟宿池边树，僧敲月下门。
过桥分野色，移石动云根。
暂去还来此，幽期不负言。

Dedicating to Li Ning's Secret Abode

A leisure abode almost has no neighbor.
A grassy path leads to a waste garden.
Birds prefer dwelling on trees near water.
A monk once knocked the door under the moon.
Beyond a bridge, there will be the wild.
Rooting in rocks, the clouds are moved.
I'll come back after leaving for a while.
The private tryst cannot be given up.

寻隐者不遇

松下问童子，言师采药去。
只在此山中，云深不知处。

Looking for a Hermit, Fail Yet

Beneath a pine I asked a boy.
Gone for herbs my teacher has.
He is certain in this mountain.
The thick clouds hide his site.

朱庆馀

Zhu Qingyu

闺意献张水部

洞房昨夜停红烛，待晓堂前拜舅姑。
妆罢低声问夫婿，画眉深浅入时无？

A Woman's Worry, Dedicated to Water Governor Zhang [1]

All night in bridal chamber the red candles burn.
She waits for the dawn to meet his parents at hall.
After doing makeup she softly asks her husband:
"Whether the painted eyebrows are fit or not? "

1. Water Governor Zhang was Zhang Ji. Zhu Qingyu wrote this poem to him before the Imperial Examination in order to know whether his learning is in line with the need of government or not.

李凭箜篌引

李贺

Li He

吴丝蜀桐张高秋，空山凝云颓不流。

江娥啼竹素女愁，李凭中国弹箜篌。

An Introduction of Li Ping's Konghou Playing [1]

In high autumn, strings of Wu and timbers of Shu are opened up. [2]
The mountains quiet down, the clouds solidify and the waters stop.
Wives from the Xiang River spot bamboos and the Virgin feels sorrow. [3]
Li Ping in the center of the world is gong to play the Konghou.

1. Konghou was a kind of harp in ancient times. Li Ping was a musician.
2. Wu and Shu are two regions.
3. Wives from Xiang River were two wives of Shun, who was a chief in early ancient times. It was said that they wept the death of Shun and their tears caused the spots of bamboos. The Virgin or Sunü（素女）was a goddess who was good at music.

昆山玉碎凤凰叫，芙蓉泣露香兰笑。
十二门前融冷光，二十三丝动紫皇。
女娲炼石补天处，石破天惊逗秋雨。

A jade in the Kunlun Mountains is broken and phoenixes yell. [4]
Hibiscuses weep with dewdrops and fragrant orchids smile.
The cold sights outside the twelve city gates melt away. [5]
The twenty-three strings make the Purple Emperor sway. [6]
At a position of the sky patched by Nüwa's processed stone, [7]
The stone cracks and the shocked sky cause the rain of autumn.

4. It was said that jades were perches of phoenixes.
5. The twelve city-gates were gates of Chang'an.
6. The twenty-three strings were strings of Konghou. Purple was a rare and noble color in ancient times. The Purple Emperor might refer to the emperor of Tang Dynasty, or the emperor of heaven.
7. In Chinese mythology, Nüwa was an important goddess who patched the sky and created human beings.

梦入神山教神妪，老鱼跳波瘦蛟舞。
吴质不眠倚桂树，露脚斜飞湿寒兔。

A mysterious hag of a mysterious mountain learns in her dream.
Old fishes jump out of the waves and a lean dragon dances deep.
The detained Wu sleeplessly leans against the cassia, [8]
Which pours dewdrops slantwise and wet the snowy hare.

8. The detained Wu was Wu Gang. He was detained by a god and punished to hew an undying cassia tree. He was a Sisyphus of China. A snow white hare accompanied him.

马诗

大漠沙如雪，燕山月似钩。
何当金络脑，快走踏清秋。

Steed

The sand of vast desert looks like the snow,
And the moon over Yan Mountains, a hook.
When will it wear the harness made of gold.
And step fast in the autumn's cool.

秋日赴阙题潼关驿楼

许浑
Xu Hun

红叶晚萧萧，长亭酒一瓢。
残云归太华，疏雨过中条。
树色随山迥，河声入海遥。
帝乡明日到，犹自梦渔樵。

On My Way to the Capital in Autumn, I Dedicate to the Towering Post Station of Tongguan[1]

At nightfall, red leaves wave and rustle.
In the long pavilion, we drink with a ladle.[2]
The last clouds return to Mount Taihua.
The sparse rain passes Mount Zhongtiao.
Colors of trees change with the mountains.
The sound of river decline with the distance.
Tomorrow I will arrive the home of Emperor.[3]
But I still dream of being a fisher and cutter.

1. Tongguan (潼关), or Tong Pass, was the east gate of the plain in which Chang'an lay. Mount Taihua,or Mount Hua (华山), lies to the southwest of Tongguan.
2. Here the long pavilion was the post station of Tongguan. Ancient Chinese usually set a short pavilion every five Li and a long pavilion every ten Li. Li is a Chinese unit of distance.
3. The home of Emperor meant Chang'an, the capital of Tang Dynasty.

杜牧
Du Mu

过华清宫

长安回望绣成堆，山顶千门次第开。
一骑红尘妃子笑，无人知是荔枝来。

Passing Through the Luxurious and Clean Palace [1]

Piles of embroidery can be viewed from Chang'an.
Countless gates on hilltops are opened one by one.
A steed's coming at dawn delights the princess.
No one knows that litchis can be sent express.

1. Sub-Empress Yang lived in the Luxurious and Clean Palace, or Huaqing Palace (华清宫) on Mount Li, which lay to the east of Chang'an. "piles of embroidery" was a metaphorical expression of Mount Li. Litchis of the southernmost China were sent to Yang by express.

江南春

千里莺啼绿映红，水村山郭酒旗风。
南朝四百八十寺，多少楼台烟雨中？

The Spring of Jiangnan [1]

Orioles sing along a thousand miles of greens dotted with reds.
Flags of wine-houses flap among watery villages and hilly towns.
Of the four hundred and eighty temples built in the Southern Dynasties,[2]
How many towers and terraces are left in the mist and rain?

1. Jiangnan is a geographic area referring to lands immediately to the south of the lower reaches of Chang Jiang.
2. Southern Dynasties (420-589) are the Song Dynasty (420-479) , the Qi Dynasty (479-502) , the Liang Dynasty (502-557) and the Chen Dynasty (557-589) .

泊秦淮

烟笼寒水月笼沙，夜泊秦淮近酒家。
商女不知亡国恨，隔江犹唱《后庭花》。

Mooring on Qinhuai [1]

The water is enveloped in the mist and the sand the moonlight.
I moor on the Qinhuai River and near a wine house at night.
Service women don't know the sorrows for the lost land.
They still sing *Flowers in Backyard* on the opposite bank.

1. The Qinhuai River flows through Nanjing, a prosperous city which was the capital of Southern Dynasties. The last emperor of Chen Dynasty produced the tone named *A Tree of Jade and Flowers in Backyard.*

赤壁

折戟沉沙铁未销，自将磨洗认前朝。
东风不与周郎便，铜雀春深锁二乔。

Red Cliff [1]

A broken halberd in the sand remains a little.
I discern its age after whetting and washing it.
If the handsome Zhou hadn't been helped by the east wind.
To Copper Finch Terrace the two beauties would be locked in.

1. Red cliff is a site of an ancient war. General Zhou Yu（周瑜）of South China and general Cao Cao （曹操）of North China confronted here and Zhou won by setting fire to Cao's troops. If Zhou had been defeated, two beauties of South China, i.e. sisters of Qiao family, would be captured and locked into the Copper Finch Terrace.

山行

远上寒山石径斜，白云生处有人家。
停车坐爱枫林晚，霜叶红于二月花。

Going Uphill

A stony path of the cool mountains goes slantingly far up.
The white clouds are born from where some abodes lie on.
I stop my vehicle and enjoy the maple woods at dusk.
Frosty leaves are more red than flowers of the second month.

清明

清明时节雨纷纷，路上行人欲断魂。
借问酒家何处有，牧童遥指杏花村。

Qingming [1]

It drizzles all along on the mournful day.
People are almost heartbroken on their way.
I ask a cowboy where I can have a drink.
He points far to huts amid flowers of pink.

1. Qingming（清明）means clean and clear. It's one term of 24 solar terms. It's a mourning day, on which Chinese people commemorate their ancestors and sweep tombs.

陈陶

Chen Tao

陇西行

誓扫匈奴不顾身，五千貂锦丧胡尘。
可怜无定河边骨，犹是春闺梦里人。

The West of Lǒng Mountains

Having swore to clean out the Huns at all costs,
Five thousand crack fighters perish in the alien sands.
It’s pitiful that the bones beside a river unsteady,
Are still the beloved in dreams of a lone lady.

锦瑟

李商隐

Li Shangyin

锦瑟无端五十弦，一弦一柱思华年。
庄生晓梦迷蝴蝶，望帝春心托杜鹃。
沧海月明珠有泪，蓝田日暖玉生烟。
此情可待成追忆，只是当时已惘然。

The Aureate Zither

Suddenly break, all strings of the aureate zither.
Each string reminds me of times when we were together.
In his dawn dream, a butterfly the thinker Zhuang changes into. [1]
At every spring, King Du sings his heart out as a cuckoo. [2]
Pearls are tears of the sea when the moon is bright.
Jades of Blue Field smoke under the warm sunlight. [3]
I can recollect, or I might meet you in the other side.
But at this moment, the griefs have no way for me to hide.

1. Zhuangzi（庄子）was a thinker in the Warring States Period.
2. It was said that Du Yu（杜宇）, the King of Shu, had changed into a cuckoo after his death and sang in every spring to remind his people to culture.
3. Blue fields, or Lantian（蓝田）, is a place producing jades.

登乐游原

向晚意不适，驱车登古原。
夕阳无限好，只是近黄昏。

Ascending the Happy Tour Upland [1]

Feeling unwell before dusk,
I drive to an antique upland.
The setting sun is so splendid,
Soon will come the deep dark.

1. Happy Tour Upland, or Leyou Upland（乐游原）was beside Chang'an.

夜雨寄北

君问归期未有期，巴山夜雨涨秋池。
何当共剪西窗烛，却话巴山夜雨时。

Writing to the North in a Rainy Night

The returning day you asked is not decided.
The autumn rain tonight is having pools filled.
When could we sit close at home with a candle.
All my moods in the Ba Mountain tonight I can tell. [1]

1. The Ba Mountain, or the Daba Mountain（大巴山）, is a mountain range of central China.

贾生

宣室求贤访逐臣，贾生才调更无伦。
可怜夜半虚前席，不问苍生问鬼神。

Mr. Jia [1]

The royal court looked for the worthies including those relegated courtiers.
Among which, Mr. Jia was incomparably excellent in his talents and virtues.
It was so sorry that the Emperor unconsciously moved his knees to approach Jia,
But his questions pointed to the ghosts and gods instead of the mortal beings.

1. Mr. Jia was Jia Yi（贾谊）. He was once relegated and recalled by Emperor Wen of Han Dynasty.

西施

家国兴亡自有时，吴人何苦怨西施。
西施若解倾吴国，越国亡来又是谁？

Xi Shi [1]

The rise or fall of a power is doomed.
Why men of Wu have Xi Shi blamed?
Even if Xi Shi caused the fall of Wu.
Whom the fall of Yue could due to?

1. Xi Shi, was one of the renowned Four Beauties of ancient China. She was said to have been sent by the king of Yue to the king of Wu, in order to undermine Wu.

自遣

得即高歌失即休，多愁多恨亦悠悠。
今朝有酒今朝醉，明日愁来明日愁。

To Free Myself

Sing high when win, and feel sad when fail.
Many worries and sorrows remain as usual.
Having some wine today, I'll be drunk today.
Having a worry tomorrow, I'll worry tomorrow.

汴河怀古

皮日休

Pi Rixiu

尽道隋亡为此河，至今千里赖通波。
若无水殿龙舟事，共禹论功不较多。

Thinking of the Ancients by the Bian River

It's well known that Sui Dynasty
Has died for this river.
But thousands of miles today
Are linked by her.
Had Emperor Yang not toured [1]
By the huge dragon boat.
His achievement can be compared
With Yu the Great.

1. Emperor Yang of Sui Dynasty（隋炀帝）accomplished the Grand Canal network. In this poem, he was compared with Yu the Great（大禹）, an Chinese mythological hero, who tamed the flood.

黄巢
Huang Chao

不第后赋菊

待到秋来九月八，我花开后百花杀。
冲天香阵透长安，满城尽带黄金甲。

Praising Golden Flowers
After Failing in the Imperial Examination

Awaiting the eighth day of the ninth month.
We bloom while the others be put to death.
The vast and high aroma overflow Chang'an.
All over the city be clad by golden armors.

焚书坑

章碣

Zhang Jie

竹帛烟销帝业虚，关河空锁祖龙居。
坑灰未冷山东乱，刘项原来不读书。

Pits for Burning Books

Bamboos and silks went up in smoke,
While the empire went down.
Mountains and rivers vainly locked
The initial dragon's court.[1]
The ash in pits was still warm,
But the eastern region began to revolt.
The leaders were Liu and Xiang,
Who had never read a book.

1. The initial dragon was Ying Zheng（嬴政）, the first Emperor of Qin Dynasty and China. He ordered to burn all books threatening his rule. After his death, Liu Bang（刘邦）and Xiang Yu（项羽）rebelled and ruined Qin Dynasty.

曹松

Cao Song

己亥岁

泽国江山入战图，生民何计乐樵苏。
凭君莫话封侯事，一将功成万骨枯。

The Year of Ji-Hai [1]

The watery south was drawn into military maps.
How could people maintain their ordinary lives.
You please don't talk about the ennoblement.
One gets fame after the death of ten thousand.

1. Chinese designate years by ten Heavenly Stems and twelve Earthly Branches. Ji is the sixth Heavenly Stem and Hai is the last Earthly Branch. The year of Ji-Hai can be calculated as 879 AD.